WALLS

Robert E. Creekmur

Set Time Publications
Chesapeake, VA

Set Time Publications
P.O. Box 6534
Chesapeake, VA 23323

ISBN-13:978-0615692548

CHAPTER 1

Dr. Carl Peterson watched the sunrise over the mountains of Guyana. Actually, when he thought about it, he wasn't sure where he was actually located. He knew he was near the border of Guyana, Suriname and Brazil, but, to tell the truth, he had crossed the border so many times he didn't know in what country he was actually standing.

Dr. Peterson was not a very sociable man. He really didn't like working or interacting with people. He was much more at ease working with inanimate objects, such as computers, machines and artifacts rather than people. Luckily, in his chosen field of archaeology, he had plenty of time to spend working with objects. However, what he hated the most about his field were the fundraisers and social events, which helped fund his projects. When he attended them he had to cater to the rich idiots who held his purse strings. He had to listen to them babble on about archaeology as if they really knew about the subject. Through it all, he had to smile and nod his head, when he really wanted to tell them how stupid they sounded.

His thoughts turned to The Search, the journey that had taken on a life of its own and all his free time for the last 10 years. Where did it all start? It seemed so long ago, he had to think about it. In the beginning, he had been a traditional scientist using standard methods and thinking like the rest of them. He had the same training and mindset as them then. Don't do this; do it this way; don't destroy this; and preserve that. That's the way he used to search for things - - the tried and true accepted way; the proven way. That was how he had worked, but there was a problem with the established methods and techniques he had been taught. They took time, and time was something Dr. Peterson felt was running out on him.

He had started out in his field as a bright young grad student, ready to conquer the world in his twenties. Years later, there he stood; a fifty five-year-old with no major accomplishments or discoveries. Maybe he could handle that if he had money for all his hard years of work, but the pitiful amount of money the University called a salary was not enough to sustain the lifestyle he envisioned for himself; the poverty level pension he had to look forward to was also an insult. No, this was not what he expected for his life. What really brought this to light for him was watching his colleagues retire. People whom he had respected and looked up to were being tossed aside and forgotten like garbage thrown out on the curb. That was not going to happen to him; he was going to make a mark for himself and profit at the same time. If he had to break every rule in the book to do it, then that's what he was going to do.

After he came to that conclusion he started looking for the big score, the one big discovery that would give him everything he wanted; wealth, fame, status, and the kind of recognition he felt he deserved. They say every major discovery has already been made; however, he reasoned there had to be something out there that nobody had even thought of or ever tried to find.

One thing he had found to be a constant was that no matter how strange or crazy a legend sounded it usually had some basis in truth. This fact seemed to be true no matter in what country it was discovered. The only questions were which legend was likely to be the most profitable and had the most likelihood of discovery.

After years of searching and research he found one that stood out. It was a story that appeared in several cultures in the same basic form. It was a story of a fabulous machine like object that supposedly could create anything the user desired. There was no explanation on how this was done or what happened to it, but elements of the same story were repeated throughout folklore. There also seemed to be a disastrous end to the whole affair. He had spent most of the last 10 years of his life looking for this object. He was thinking about all this when his thoughts were interrupted by the shouts of Carlos, his guide and hired man. He was yelling and running toward him frantically. What now?

CHAPTER 2

Carlos ran up to the Dr., out of breath and panting. "Well, what is it?" said Peterson. He was impatiently waiting for Carlos to catch his breath. Finally, Carlos opened his mouth and said, "I found something." The Dr. was still a little irritated at him.

"Found what?"

"A piece of curved metal."

Peterson began to think. What is Carlos talking about?

During The Search, he had been led to the cave sight. He never told Carlos or anyone else what he really was trying to discover. Dr. Peterson didn't trust anyone with that information. He only told Carlos he was searching for any artifacts from ancient cultures that may have lived in the area. He instructed Carlos to look for anything that looked man made and not natural.

"Show it to me," said Peterson. He followed his guide to the cave entrance. As they entered the cave, they passed the roar of the generators. They powered the lights strung at neat intervals along the corridor they had opened into the nearby hill. They had blasted open this passageway with dynamite. The corridor stopped at the end with a solid wall of dirt and rock. It opened there to become a much wider area as a result of them digging in all directions. Dr.

Peterson smiled as he thought about how his colleagues would have reacted if they knew he was using dynamite at an excavation site. They would say he could have been destroying valuable objects by what they would call his reckless use of explosives. Well, he didn't care about that; all the Dr. was after was one thing, money.

"Well, where is it?" Dr. Peterson snapped.

"Over there," said Carlos.

In the harsh lighting and dark shadows cast by the bright lights, he saw something. It was bright and shiny, barely sticking out of the wall, which marked the end of the cave. Carlos had come in early and had been scratching around. Peterson pulled the flashlight from his belt and took a closer look. It was curved, metallic, and definitely not natural. It had to be manmade, but something was odd about what he saw. It was shiny, too shiny and reminded him of chrome or stainless steel. Those are both modern metals. Nothing like that could have existed thousands of years ago. This could be another dead end, but how could something made during modern times get way in here and in the time period of this layer of earth?

Whatever it was, it was there in front of him, and now he had another problem. Carlos was standing there seeing everything Dr. Peterson was seeing. Maybe now is the time to get rid of him according to plan, Peterson thought. But it may be too soon; after all, Peterson didn't know what he had, if anything yet. He had to get a close look at what was covered up in the cave wall without anyone else around. Maybe it is time to get rid of his helper while he is still in the dark.

"It's nothing; just a piece of shiny ore in an odd shape. It looks like metal, but it's not. I've seen this before. Come on, let's get out of here," urged Dr. Peterson.

The Dr. had to quickly get Carlos away; he had seen enough. Perhaps he would fall for the cover story that the Dr. had planned in advance. Peterson's mind was racing as they walked out of the cave entrance; past the generators to the tents they called a base camp.

"You know Carlos, I hate to tell you, but I guess this is as good a time as any. This last false alarm is just about it for this year. I have just about run out of funding. I was holding on, thinking we might get a lucky break; that we would find something at this last dig that would get me more funding, but it hasn't worked out that way. I'm going to have to shut down here, pack up, and head back to the states. I'm going to pay you today, and in the morning, you need to go on and head back to your village."

Carlos had a sad disappointed look on his face.

"Well, whatever you say, Dr. Peterson. What about the equipment and the tents, who is going to help you with them?"

"Don't worry about that. I'll just get on the radio and call for my people in the capitol to come help me. Don't worry about me. Just go home, and take care of that pretty wife of yours and be with your children," directed Dr. Peterson. With that, he let out a big smile. He quickly suppressed it. I don't want to overdo the acting, he thought. Carlos had been with him long enough to know that smiling is out of character for Peterson.

Later that night, Peterson lay in his tent trying to sleep, but unable to sleep. The incessant flapping of the sides of his tent in the brisk wind didn't help. Did he really find something? After all these years

8

and all the money he has spent, could he really have hit pay dirt? He wanted so badly to have a closer look at what he saw, and what he saw was probably only a small part of the whole object. The rest of it was underneath all that earth, but of two things he was certain. Whatever it was, it was deliberately put there, and it had to be manmade. After that, all bets were off on anything else about it. He couldn't stop thinking about it. Sometimes, he hated the way his mind worked. His mind was always thinking, always hashing and rehashing things, pouring over thoughts. While everyone around him seemed relaxed and at rest with his or her thoughts, he was always thinking. At times like this, he almost envied them. If he could stop thinking so much maybe he could sleep. After what seemed like hours of tossing and turning, Dr. Peterson finally fell asleep.

The next day was frustrating. Peterson was eager to get to the find, but Carlos seemed agonizingly slow packing up his gear and heading for home. Peterson's nerves were on edge and he had to hold back his temper. Will he just leave so I can get some idea of what I found? It was afternoon before he was finally able to wave goodbye to Carlos as he disappeared over the hill north of the camp. Finally, he thought. Peterson rushed to the cave to investigate what he had found.

The next day, Peterson stood with his hands on his hips, staring at the object he had dug out of the wall. There it was, gleaming in the bright lights of the cave. Where in the world did this thing come from, or did it come from this world at all? It consisted of all smooth, curved angles. There were no seams or panels on it. It had the appearance of being a single piece of metal and was about five feet long. It reminded him of a bathtub made of stainless steel, but high on one end - - maybe five feet tall. Its height rapidly dropped down until it was about six inches tall on the other end. There were no knobs, dials, controls, or panels on the thing. He couldn't find any gauges, instruments, writing, or instructions on it. This couldn't be anything functional. After all, any machine, no matter what kind it was, had to have controls or something on it that actually moved.

What a disappointment. Sure it was remarkable that he found something like this, which seemed to have been here for thousands of years. Anyone else would have been ecstatic about a find like this, but he was looking for more. He may get some fame and money off this, but Peterson wanted it all. He wanted the big score he had dreamed about all these years - - unlimited riches and wealth, not the limited amount of money and fame he would get from this. It would probably wind up in a museum somewhere, or, even worse yet, the government might confiscate it. After all, they might not want the public to know about this until they figured out its origin. In fact, they may never want it revealed to the public. It all depended on what they found out. Think of the ramifications, if it turned out this was made thousands of years ago with technology it appears we don't even have today. Oh stop it, he thought. Who cares about all this speculation? All I care about is the money.

While staring at and examining the thing, it occurred to him the taller end did appear to be a seat or at least was shaped like an area where a person would sit. Also, the areas on both sides did look somewhat like armrests. Peterson approached it and ran his hands along the shiny skin. It was cold to the touch; not just cool, but actually cold. He had noticed that a little earlier, while he was brushing and cleaning the left over dirt and dust from the thing. But he hadn't touched it with his bare skin before. Odd, it didn't seem that cold in the cave. He stepped up into the thing and stood in front of the seat. Well, let's see if anything is going to happen.

Peterson sat down, wiggled in the seat and waited, but nothing happened. Well show me something, he thought. However, no vibration, no humming or anything else occurred, absolutely nothing happened. It was basically sitting there just like it was before with no reaction. The only thing he noticed noteworthy was the cold coming from it. It was a penetrating cold. The coldness in this strange, unidentified object went through his clothes and was starting to numb his skin. I need to get this thing out of here and into the sunlight, he thought. This thing is just too cold to work with the way it is now.

But now he had another problem. He had dragged it a few feet out of the wall by himself, but now he realized he had to drag it at least 500 feet, to get it out of the cave. In his haste to get rid of Carlos he hadn't given any thought to how he would get the thing out of the cave.

How stupid; I have got to figure a way to get it out. While he was scratching his head, thinking on that, another thought hit him. While he had examined every inch of the thing, he couldn't call it a machine because it doesn't seem to do anything; he had never examined the bottom of it. What else have I forgotten? Am I getting old, lazy or just senile? Well, the best way to get a quick look at the bottom is just to try lifting up one end, Peterson reasoned within himself.

Peterson carefully grabbed the bottom of what he figured was the front end and lifted. To his great surprise, it was amazingly light. While it looked to him to weigh at least 400 pounds, it felt like it weighed only about 100 pounds. While he was able to lift it, perhaps a foot, what he saw on the bottom didn't look any different than the rest of it. Wait a minute, he thought. There seems to be a slight knob or protrusion under here. He touched it, and to his amazement, heard a slight humming sound. It was almost like the sound of a small electric motor. An opening suddenly appeared underneath, and a round chrome ball appeared from inside this unidentified object. He dropped the end in shock and jumped away. What in the world is happening?

The Dr. stood there, with his heart racing, staring at this thing. It was now on the ground, tilted with one end higher than the other. A chrome ball about three inches in diameter was coming out of the bottom front end, raising that end off the ground. The ball was attached to a short shaft and it reminded him of the end of a huge ballpoint pen. So it does do something after all. That means this thing was meant to be moved. Where are the other wheels?

He approached it slowly and carefully. He lifted up the other end and found another protrusion and pressed it. There was the same sound again; however, Peterson didn't drop the end as before but held it up. This time two balls came out of it. They both looked like the ball on the front end. He gently lowered it to the ground. He pushed the front of the object and noticed the front wheel pivoted, but the rear wheels only rolled to accommodate the front. So it was steered by the front end, and the rear went wherever the front was aimed.

Peterson pushed it, and it rolled pretty well. There was some difficulty with its movement because of the dirt and rocks on the cave floor. But, all in all, he would have no real problem getting it out of the cave by himself. He began the long push to the entrance and the welcome warmth of the sun.

After about 30 minutes of pushing and pausing to catch his breath, he stopped about 50 feet outside the entrance.

Now, let me see what's here. Peterson got down on his hands and knees to get a better look at the bottom. Wait a minute; I see something.

There seemed to be lines on the underside almost like sketching or drawings. He put the object down and picked up a loose wooden board that was lying nearby. He used it to prop up the device so he could study whatever was there. His jaw dropped at what he saw. There, in the light of day, was a drawing of a man sitting in this thing, who had something on his head that looked like a helmet.

A helmet, he thought? There's no helmet with this thing. Could I have missed something? He turned around and made a mad dash for the cave entrance.

After 20 minutes of digging, in the area behind the original location of the unidentified object, Peterson stood at the rear wall holding in his hand the helmet he saw in the sketch. The helmet had a stainless steel appearance similar to the metal on the larger object. For the first time, he started to think of it as a machine.

It must do something if it has a helmet to go with it, unless it's nothing but some sort of fancy go-cart or soapbox racer. "What a ridiculous thought," he said aloud to himself. Who would go to all the trouble to make something like this to roll down a hill; and if they did, it had to be the most poorly designed racer in history. Who would race in a three-wheel configuration for starters? There was no steering capability, he could see - - no wheel, no handles, and no controls whatsoever.

Peterson put the crazy idea out of his head and continued to examine the helmet. After further examination, he saw no wires, connections, or anything on this thing. There was nothing but a smooth metal surface inside and outside. It all seemed to be made out of one piece of solid metal, just like the machine. There seems to be no function to this helmet. Maybe it's some sort of ritual involved with wearing it.

He walked out of the cave, helmet in hand. The sight that greeted him startled him. In his haste to run to the cave in search of the helmet, he forgot to put the machine down. Upon exiting the cave, there it was, still propped up by the board. This thing could have fallen and been easily damaged the way he left it. He walked over to it and put the helmet down. He grabbed the end, kicked the board out and put the end on the ground. His hair stood on end. Is this thing vibrating?

CHAPTER 3

Peterson held his hand on the surface of the machine. It definitely was vibrating. It was barely perceivable, but it was vibrating. There was a low humming sound along with the vibration. Peterson noticed something else; it wasn't cold anymore but had warmed up from the sunlight. Could sunlight have something to do with this?

A sense of apprehension came over him. With what kind of power was he dealing? The thought came to him; was he way out of his league? He was tampering with things he didn't understand. Maybe he could never understand what he had found. It was one thing accepting the idea of this in theory, but now he was facing the reality of this machine sitting in front of him. The reality of it, if it was the machine of legend, made him pause. But then he snapped back to his normal self-confident state of mind.

I can handle it. After all, this is what I have been looking for all these years and I'm sure not going to stop now.

With his confidence restored, Peterson approached the machine carefully, helmet in hand. Let me not be too hasty. He gave it a slow walk around, visually inspecting for any changes he hadn't noticed. He saw no change in appearance. It looked the same as before. Well, maybe it's time to sit on it.

His pulse was racing. Then, he realized he still had the helmet in his hands. *Let me at least try to preserve some semblance of a scientific method.*

He went to one of the storage tents and emptied out an old metal box he knew was there. It had a hinged lid on it, and this suited his purpose. He put the helmet in the box, closed the lid, and took the box deep inside the cave. *That should prevent the helmet from having any effect on the machine when I sit on it, or will it?* He came back to the machine and stood beside it. *Well, I guess this is it. Let me see how it acts without the helmet first. Here goes nothing.*

Peterson took a deep breath, climbed on and waited and waited and waited. After five or ten minutes of this, he thought to himself, *nothing happened. Oh, he could still feel it vibrating as before, but nothing else. Well, if nothing else it will make a good body massager.*

Peterson looked up at the sun. It was late afternoon, and the sun was low in the sky. Less than an hour of good sunlight was left in the day. *I'm tired from all this exertion. I need to stop for the day.*

He realized he needed to at least cover up his find to hide it from prying eyes. He got off the object, and went to get a tarp he remembered seeing in one of the supply tents. To his relief, it covered it completely. *At least no one will be able to see it without lifting the tarp.*

Just before leaving, he stuck his hand under the tarp and felt the surface. Just as he thought, the vibrations stopped when the tarp covered it and blocked the sun. He went back into the cave and retrieved the box with the helmet inside. *This stays with me. I have a feeling nothing works without this. This is never going to leave my side.*

Peterson returned to his tent to prepare a hasty meal. He was exhausted and hungry. He ate his food but got no satisfaction out of it, barely tasting it. After all, his mind was occupied by a million thoughts. All his thoughts were on his find, what was in store for him tomorrow, and what the future held if this thing turned out to be real. He played in his mind, repeatedly, the day's events. Did he miss anything, was it something he overlooked? What will he do if this thing actually does what the legend says? What will he ask it to create, gold? Gold weighs a lot. How would he get it out of the middle of nowhere by himself? The more he thought about it, the more he realized how unprepared he was to actually handle his discovery. Later, the Dr. settled in to another long, fitful night of sleep. With his mind full of thoughts, he was tossing and turning all night. When this is all over, I'm going to take a long vacation. After what seemed like hours, he was finally able to go to sleep.

The next day, the sun shined through the cracks in the tent, waking him up with its warmth. He overslept from lack of sleep and exhaustion. He got up, stuck his head out of the tent and looked in the direction of his find. It was still there; he could tell by the shape of the tarp the machine was still underneath it. No one had come in by night and stolen his find from him. Furious at himself for sleeping so late, he hurriedly washed and put on his clothes. He wasn't in the mood for it, but he prepared and ate a quick breakfast. I may need the energy, he thought. This day is too important to waste making bad decisions just because I didn't have anything to eat. How stupid, in the 21st century, man still has to eat to use his mind and body effectively!

He tossed the finished plate and utensils aside, got up and went looking for a notepad. It's time I

17

started doing this right. From now on I'm recording my research on the machine.

He found a pad and ink pen among his belongings. He retrieved the helmet from the box and went over to the machine. After a worried look around him in all directions, he put the pad and helmet down. He went to the tarp, took another look around for any unwelcome prying eyes, and removed the tarp.

The sun was at a low angle in the sky because it was still early morning, but, after only a few seconds, the machine began to vibrate. The Dr. made a note of this observation. Nearly instantaneous power generation when touched by sunlight, but there is a delay of a few seconds, he wrote. I wonder how much power this thing is generating now. In fact I wonder how much power it's capable of generating. No way to tell, he thought. It has no gauges and I don't have any equipment to measure power.

The more he thought about it, he really didn't bring anything with him to test or measure anything about this thing. What's wrong with me? He realized he wasn't prepared at all for this discovery. Why wasn't I ready? He could only come to the conclusion that he must have not really believed he would find it. What a sobering thought indeed. After all the time and money he had spent, deep down inside him, he really didn't think he would find anything. Well, enough of all this, let me get down to the task at hand.

He climbed up and sat down on the seat, helmet in hand. He felt the same vibration throughout his body as before. So far, so good, he thought. Now, let's see what happens when I put on the helmet and test if it interacts with the machine. He slowly raised the helmet, paused and gingerly put it on his

18

head.

From thousands of years of slumber, the mind probe on his head slowly awakened. It was in sunlight, the main source of its power, and it recognized that. It also recognized something else. It was in proximity to a brain. The whole reason for its existence was nearby, and, not only nearby, but in perfect position to scan, according to the program. You, see it didn't think, have thoughts or emotions like us. It only did what it was programmed to do eons ago by unknown beings. Its job was to probe the mind and transmit whatever the mind wanted to the machine. Then the machine's job was to change energy to matter and create whatever the mind using it wanted.

The programming was to be followed; of course there was no chance that it wouldn't. After all, a machine can only do what it is designed to do; however, there was a problem. The mind using it was not the type of mind for which it was designed. Oh, it would look pretty much the same to the casual observer. It would appear about the same size, shape and makeup as the long forgotten original users, but there were differences in which area of the brain controlled different functions of the body. There were also differences in which area of the brain controlled dreams, nightmares, emotions, desires, love and hate. There also was a big difference in the ability to handle the type of power this machine could generate. The human mind was near its limitations handling the normal power settings and ill- equipped to handle any increase above that.

During its scan, the mind probe noticed the readings didn't appear normal or average; however, the result of the scan was within limits. Even though some of the readings were on the outermost edge of the perimeters, and barely within limits, the averages of the readings were within limits.

Dr. Peterson initially noted no change at all with the helmet on his head. Then he felt a noticeable increase in vibrations from the machine. He also slowly realized there was a slight tingling all around his head. It was nothing big, but he felt it from all directions. Then the sensation stopped coming from all directions and centered on two areas of his head. It was almost as if something had mapped his whole head, then settled on the areas in which it was interested. It was a soothing sensation, nothing alarming about it. This reminds me of a computer at startup, he thought. It's probably running a type of program that starts the same way every time. The Dr. was relaxed and felt at ease. He reasoned that, if there was any problem, all he had to do was remove the helmet and everything would shut down. In fact, maybe I had better test it now.

He quickly removed the helmet, and the sensation was gone. The vibrations from the machine also quickly dropped down to a low level. But he noticed a fluorescent looking glow on the entire surface of the helmet. It was there for a split second, and then it faded. It was like the cutting off of a light. It must have been doing that the whole time it was on, but I couldn't see that with it on my head.

He went to his tent and got his mirror he used for shaving, returned to the machine, and propped it up so he could see his head. Now I can watch the helmet while I'm wearing it.

He made a quick note of his findings in his log. He was starting to feel better about his tests, now that he was recording his actions in the log. Confident that he had control of his experiment, he put the helmet back on to resume his tests.

20

The mind probe reactivated and reestablished its connection with the machine. An error message was sent out. Its programming was telling it something was wrong. Since only qualified users were authorized to use the machine, there should not be an interruption in the data stream so soon after start. It went through its startup error checklist in milliseconds. The data stream stopped prematurely. A list of options was accessed:

1. The user saw something wrong and took the helmet off.
If this was true, he would have made adjustments before starting again. This didn't happen, so #1 was eliminated.

2. There is a program error.
Diagnostics run on software and no error found. #2 eliminated.

3. There is a hardware problem in the mind probe or the machine.
Diagnostics run on both and no problem found. #3 eliminated.

4. There is signal interference between the mind probe and the user brain.

The most likely error is signal interference: Cause unknown
Corrective action: Boost power output to the helmet.

With that decision by an unthinking machine, the faith of mankind was sealed.

CHAPTER 4

Dr. Peterson was relaxed and feeling good about how things were going in the experiment. Then suddenly, there was a huge surge of energy from the helmet. His head began to pound and his ears began to ring. He saw lights and spots in front of his eyes. He tried to lift his hands and remove the helmet from his head, but his arms were like lead. It was as if the armrests were pulling them down and holding them in place. The pain was unbearable. Fear gripped him. What's happening? I can't believe I'm going to die like this in this godforsaken place.

In the middle of his pain, he felt overwhelming rage and anger that his end was coming like this. The last thing he remembered was hearing his own voice yelling a loud primitive scream. Then there was blackness and silence as he lost consciousness.

The machine continued on with its program. It had no concern with the state of the body sitting on it. Its only concern, if you could call it that, was for the brain with which it was in contact. The brain was operating and suffering no damage. So it continued on with its purpose, to give the brain whatever it wanted.

The readings however were confusing, a little odd and a little different than normal. It repeated its scan several times and probed twice as long as usual.

It didn't get a clear request for anything, so it went to the secondary program. The secondary program was simple: when lacking a clear request, give the user brain what the machine determined it desired. It determined this by using the data it took from the user. This one had heightened amounts of extreme emotions. It sensed rage, anger and hatred. This user had an almost dislike of its own kind. This brain had a desire for unlimited power with no concern for the effect of this power on anyone or the world around him.

If the machine's memory banks had not been degraded from eons of neglect, extremes of temperature, pressure and lack of maintenance, it would have noticed something familiar about the readings it was receiving. But since that part of it was not working at 100 percent, it didn't notice it recorded similar readings once, thousands of years ago.

All of its resources were being trained on the problem at hand. As a machine, it did not think of morals or right or wrong. Without hesitation it cranked up its power, the unlimited and immeasurable power of the sun. Its internal power gauges went up to their maximum readings. It began to pull and create the maximum power it was capable of generating from the sun. Energy to matter - - that was the method it used. The air around it was pulsating with energy. Arches of electricity went in all directions. The smell of ozone filled the air. The stench of the ozone would have filled the nostrils of anyone in the area, but there was no one there to smell it, except the unconscious Dr. Peterson. Slowly, a shape began to form. It was a huge, bizarre shape that defied the imagination - - something completely unnatural.

It was 15 minutes after the machine had finished its work that the Dr. awoke. He was dizzy and his head throbbed. What happened? Well, at least this infernal thing didn't kill me. He realized he still had the helmet on and quickly snatched it off, tossing it aside. It tried to kill me and it almost did. His eyes were bleary and out of focus. He looked around and almost jumped out of the seat. He couldn't see clearly, but there was a huge, dark shape standing in front of him blocking the sun. He peered at it with his eyes partly closed. He closed them and was almost afraid to open them again. He slowly opened them and as the shape began to come into focus he saw the unbelievable. A huge statue of an animal was there in front of him. Where did it come from? This infernal machine must have conjured up this statue.

He dismounted the machine and slowly walked around the statue. It was so life like it almost looked alive, but it was completely unnatural. It looked like a prehistoric four-legged dinosaur, but unlike any he had ever seen in any textbook. Its head was tremendous, at least twice the size of a T- Rex. By the shape of its mouth, if it was real he could tell it would have been filled with carnivorous teeth. This was no plant eater. There were scales all over his body. They looked like some type of defensive armor similar to that on a triceratops, but much more complicated. It also had webbing between its toes like something with which a sea creature would use to swim. The feet had large and menacing claws, the kind that looked like they were made for ripping open flesh and disemboweling other animals with one swipe. He walked to the tail and around to the other side. The scales were everywhere. Different sizes and shapes covered every inch of the animal. What a ridicules monstrosity. Why would this machine go to all this trouble to create such a useless and obscene work of art?

The Dr. slowly looked over the entire statue. As he raised his gaze to look at its head he noticed something odd. It almost looked as if it was smiling - - well, about as much of a smile as you could put on an animal. There were more things that looked wrong. Chills went up his spine. There's something strange about the eyes. When Dr. Peterson started walking from the front, he could have sworn they were looking forward. Now, they seemed to be pointed toward the rear. In fact, they were pointed directly at him. Then he noticed something else. Its diaphragm was moving as if it was breathing, no not as if it was breathing. It is breathing. This is no statue; it's alive and staring directly at me.

The creature had come to the realization of its existence, but it felt weak. It was barely able to stand. It stood motionless. It felt the heat of the sun on its skin, which seemed comforting to it. It could feel its strength increasing by the minute and sensed it had something to do with the sun. The creature started to look around and observe his environment. There was a puny looking creature sleeping on something directly in front of him. The little creature was too small to be of any importance or danger to him, but somehow he sensed extreme danger from this little creature. He became alarmed and stepped back a few steps at the sight of the puny thing. He didn't understand why, but he knew instinctively that this little creature or its kind was the only thing he had to fear, the only animal that could harm him.

Yes, the huge creature could think. In fact, it was very intelligent for an animal; however, there was a paradox. It really wasn't an animal. It looked like one, but it wasn't; it was an unnatural creation. Its

25

mind was part human and part animal. Its body was a combination of different species, some of which were extinct. Parts of him were also found nowhere in nature. They were all held together by fantastic amounts of energy.

More thoughts were coming to the creature as his strength increased. He was feeling stronger and more and more confident. His hybrid mind told him he was more powerful than anything that could oppose him. In fact, he was sure now nothing could stop him. This world was his for the taking. He would rule here and he had contempt for any other life on this planet. Still, there was the puzzle of this puny little creature in front of him. He had sensed overwhelming danger from him initially. He could still sense danger, but the stronger he grew the less danger he felt from him. After all, he could crush him with one toe if he desired to kill him. How much harm could he cause? His attitude changed from fear to amusement. He watched him as he awoke and decided to stand motionless and watch him as he got up and walked around his body. He watched him as he came to realize he was alive. He's not very smart, thought the large creature.

The Dr. was shocked beyond all bounds. How was it possible that this huge living abomination was standing in front of him? He created him from the machine obviously, but how? He never asked or dreamed of anything like this. He also never considered this machine or any machine could create life. He only thought it possible that it could create inanimate objects like silver or gold. What kind of knowledge could make something like this? Enough of this, he thought as his mind was starting to wander again. Warning signals were beginning to come into

26

his head. He was standing too close to the animal. One step from one of its huge feet and he would be nothing but a red spot of blood and raw meat on the ground. He slowly stepped backward from the thing. It made no moves but kept its eyes fixed on him. After moving a respectable distance away, he felt a little better. It had made no threatening moves toward him. In fact it seemed docile and non-aggressive. The Dr. began to feel better about the whole situation. I created him. That logically means I should have control of him. He probably is just waiting for me to tell him what to do. I can handle this. Dr. Peterson swallowed his fear and pulled out his most confident voice. With a stern loud voice he said, "You, go over there by the stream and stand there."

The creature was shocked and amazed. This puny little man was ordering him around and he didn't like it. His first instinct was to kill him, but he decided to play along with him. He had to learn more about this little creature. He sensed already by his tone and demeanor that this life form must be the dominant life form on this world. This little animal actually expected him to cater to his commands. All right, he would play along for now. He walked over to the stream and stood.

More and more memory was being retrieved in his mind. He didn't understand or know it, but he shared memory with the Dr. and fragments of memory in the machine of long ago human contact. Now he knew this little animal was called man. Now he felt something else, he knew now he hated him and his kind. It was a mixture of hatred and contempt. He hated everything about man, his works, his arrogance, his world and, most of all, his entire attitude that he was in charge of this world. Now he knew his purpose, he had to destroy the works of man

27

and what man held dear, and then bring him under submission. Then he would make man bow down to him and admit he was the ruler of this world, not some god, man or government, but him.

Dr. Peterson was pleased. This creature may be huge and menacing, but he had control of it. It understood and obeyed him. He was just a huge dog in a way. He created him by accident, but now that it is here he has control of him. It made him feel powerful.

But now what am I going to do with him? He's huge; I just can't let him roam around. I can't hide him forever either. Out here in the middle of nowhere I don't have a problem. But, when I take it near people they will panic when they first see him.

He thought of the movie about a giant ape that was taken from the jungle to the big city and put on exhibit. They were trying to make money off it. Now that money making scheme didn't work out very well. That was because they didn't have control of the ape, he thought, well I do.

"Well since you seem to understand me, move over there beside that tent and sit down."

The creature obediently walked over to the tent and sat down on its belly. It looked somewhat like a camel would look when it sits on the ground. But this was no camel and he had just about had enough of this game and the little man ordering him around. More thoughts and memories from the man were coming to the creature now. This man was from a place called the United States. It was one of the more powerful nations on this world. One of the reasons they were so powerful was they were in some kind of alliance with a country called Ashanti which gave them cheap oil. Oil seemed to be the life blood of these people and something they valued almost more than anything.

He could visualize the makeup of this world in his mind. It was mostly water but there were landmasses where most of the humans lived. The names and their arrangement were coming clear. There was Africa, Europe, South America and others. The humans had weapons. He could see that clearly from the little man's memory. Their war machines and weapons gave them a sense of security and made them feel nothing could challenge them. He tried to understand how their weapons and war machines worked. But all he had to go by was the puny man's understanding of them. Unfortunately he didn't really understand how they worked; he only knew that they worked. Well, how they worked didn't really make any difference to the creature. Anything they had was designed to be effective against humans, not him. Instinctively he had no fear of anything man had invented.

The doctor felt it was time to make sure the creature knew who was boss.

"You, come here," he barked.

Deep inside the bowels of the creature, anger rose up. His throat began to tremble in rage. He wouldn't be talked to any more in that manner.

"COME HERE?"

The words shook the ground. Then there was dead silence. Both he and the little man stood motionless.

Where did that come from? It came from me. I can talk, reasoned the creature.

Peterson was in amazement. He just heard the creature speak words. The Dr. was so shocked at the new event he didn't even notice the tone of its voice.

Peterson thought to himself: Was he just

mimicking me or did he really know what he was saying? I better probe this and find out. The scientist in him was coming out and this was getting interesting now.

"What are you?" asked the Dr.

No response came from the creature. It just stared at him. Peterson knew it was folly to ascribe human emotions to animals, but the creature seemed as surprised as he that it could talk.

"Do you understand what I am saying?" asked Peterson. It nodded its head yes. So it's not just mimicking me, it can think, understand and talk. These are traits never exhibited in any animal. I need more answers.

"Where are you from?" "And speak this time," ordered Dr. Peterson.

Deep inside the creature's brain, that triggered something. More and more fragments of memory were coming together and connecting. Much of it didn't make sense. For some reason, it blurted out, "MY HOME IS OFF SCOTHLAND," to Peterson's question. He was as surprised as the little man with what came out of his mouth.

What did that mean, the Dr. thought? That didn't make any sense at all. Let me try a different question. He then said aloud, "maybe you're not as smart as I thought."

Anger arose in the creature when he heard that comment. He was tired of this game; it was time to end it all. He roared and moved toward the Dr. in a rapid fashion. The ground trembled with each step. Alarmed, the Dr. turned and started to run.

"What have I done?" he yelled.

Only a short distance was between them and suddenly he was upon Peterson. One quick swat with one of its massive paws and the Dr. was up and into its mouth. With two or three crunches and a swallow, so ended the life of Dr. Carl Peterson.

One thing the Dr. had forgotten, and all men have in fact forgotten, is we have fooled ourselves with all our education and higher learning. We look at all our accomplishments and attainment of knowledge over thousands of years. We pride ourselves at having reached a level where we can control our environment and just about anything we want around us, except maybe the weather. There is one thing, however, that we have never controlled – we've never been able to gain power over the deep inner thoughts of the mind. The wild, primitive, subconscious thoughts and impulses passed down from unknown thousands of years are still there. We don't even recognize or notice they are still there. We have trained ourselves over time to control our actions, but the thoughts are always present. They are buried deep in our minds. Now, they have been unleashed with unlimited power, bringing to life an unfolding of nightmares. They have brought to life a creature from the id. Not only is it birthed with all of the worst characteristics of a deeply flawed man. But, it is also birthed with the worst characteristics of all of us. The harmful impulses, traits and yearnings we have learned to suppress through thousands of years of civilization, have now been let loose.

Now on to bigger and more important things, thought the creature. He turned to walk away, but something was signaling danger to him. He took a quick look around. The man was gone and he didn't see any more men in the area. What could it be?

He couldn't understand it, but the machine, which was still intact, created him and also had the power to destroy him. To put it a different way it could change matter back to energy as easily as it could change energy to matter. The machine was now the greatest danger. Slowly realizing the machine was the danger, he pounced on it crushing it with his tremendous weight and the force of its attack. Over and over he pounded it until the only thing left was a flat slab of metal. He picked it up with his mouth and with a flick of his head tossed it into the nearby river. He noticed a small curved piece of metal the little man had on his head when he sat on the machine. One stomp of his foot was all that was needed to flatten it. A swat of his paw and the helmet went sailing through the air into the river to join the machine. The creature let loose a great roar of satisfaction. He had vanquished his enemies and there was nothing left to do here. It was time to leave, but he wasn't ready yet for mankind to know he was here. He would swim down the nearby river and use it to cover his escape to the sea.

He entered the river, but at this end it wasn't deep enough to cover his entire body. His head still protruded out of the water, so he waited until dark to start his journey. He knew the closer he got to the ocean the deeper the water would get, until he could swim unnoticed by humans. After an hour or so of waiting it was finally dark enough for him to safely travel with his head exposed and the creature started on his way.

CHAPTER 5

The President of the United States, John Logan, stood looking out of his window in the Oval Office. He was waiting for the start of a meeting he had called between himself, the Chairman of the Joint Chiefs of Staff, General Mark Hartsfield and the Secretary of State, Clarence Adams. He could have called others but these were the two he wanted to talk with now. He had developed a rapport with these two and he trusted their advice more than any of his other cabinet members or advisers. He was however, getting a little impatient waiting for them. They weren't late, but he was hoping they would come a little early so he could get this over with and go play golf.

"Why does everything around here take so long? Why does everything seem to happen so slowly here?" the President said to himself. He was a man in a hurry. President Logan had been in office for a little over a year and a half now and he felt like he was just beginning to hit his stride. All of the unsure and uncertain feelings he had about performing as President were gone.

He wasn't really interested in domestic policy. The field he was interested in was foreign policy especially fixing old headaches between countries that had lingered around seemingly forever. He wanted to change the world and go down in history books as accomplishing things no other President had done. The military side of things, for example, he deferred to others. He left that to the experts and took their advice on things like war and weapons.

His biggest accomplishment, so far, was fulfilling his campaign promise to bring peace to the Middle East. Most of his advisers had tried to talk him out of making that his primary campaign promise, but he had insisted on keeping it in his campaign. They thought it was too hard a nut to crack, especially for a first term President. But, he had pulled it off. He had brokered a seven year peace treaty between Israel and the Arab states. Well, he had not really brokered it, other countries were involved, but he was a motivating force behind it. It was something that almost seemed impossible to people at the time. In fact, it almost seemed impossible to him when he first pushed for it. It was the product of very difficult negotiations. The Israelis were definitely not in favor of it, but he finally used his ace in the hole at the end. His ace was threatening withdrawal of support for Israel.

At this point in history, no one was standing with Israel. Only the United States stood between Israel and destruction. The U.S. had been using its veto power and influence in the United Nations for years to thwart any resolutions that were unfavorable to Israel and had taken plenty of heat for it. This country had paid a big price in his mind for the support of Israel, and what were we getting out of it? All we were doing was losing money and giving them foreign aid. It's true we were selling the Israelis weapons and making a good profit off of sales. But every time the U.S. sold the Israelis weapons, we lost points in some other area of the world, especially with the Arabs. Furthermore, as Logan was so fond of saying in private, "there is a heck of a lot more Arabs than Israelis." President Logan was used to arm wringing. He had learned his trade well from long years in the senate. But the Israelis were the hardest nuts he had ever run into. Even when he threw down his ace in the hole, threatening withdrawal of support, they still wouldn't give in at first. He had them and they must have known he had them. The United States was the only major power supporting them that they had left in the world, and they still wouldn't sign the treaty. Only when he agreed to limit it to a seven-year trial period and promised to come to their aid if they were seriously attacked would the stubborn Israelis give in and agree to sign. Even now they are still probably trying to look for a way out of it, Logan thought, because after the first seven years it has to be renewed for another seven years, but they did sign it in the end.

Here in the second year of the treaty, things seemed to be going fine. There had not been any major incidents between the countries involved, except for a few maverick fanatics on the Arab side that still can't accept that the war was over. They still kept making plots and continued trying to attack Israel. There were a few cross border incidents, but the Israeli government had shown tremendous restraint and didn't automatically retaliate at each instance. The Arab governments, especially the Palestinian government, were suppressing these plotters in a way that couldn't be done in most western democracies. The Arabs had not only instantly arrested anyone they even thought were planning to attack Israel; they had retaliated against the families of those involved in plots. This was something they had never done. This had a chilling effect on those who didn't mind dying themselves, but they didn't want their family to die or suffer because of them. The family's homes were destroyed and the people disappeared never to be seen again. If they were dead or put in concentration camps somewhere, no one seemed to know. The President didn't even know, and told the Secretary of State, "I don't want to know." Whatever they were doing, it seemed to be working. But the President felt he needed to keep his eye on this thing, after all his stamp was on this. The world press was saying it was his deal. Even though the whole world was behind it, his label was on it. This was considered his treaty.

        With the implementation of this treaty, the U.S. was finally able to get the world off its back because of the country's dogged support of Israel. We were able to pull all our troops out of the Middle East and stop hemorrhaging all that money. Because of our good will with the Arabs, the War on Terror had ended. We had no more fears of planes crashing into buildings or any other kind of attack. The removal of our troops and the peace treaty with Israel ended the claimed reason for the terrorist attacks, our support of Israel, and our troops on Arab lands. The few fanatics who refused to stop trying to attack the West were dealt with by the Arab side the same as they did with the ones who tried to attack Israel.

        We now had a lucrative trade with all the Arab countries. After we got the treaty done, they started to buy American goods in mass. In fact they seemed to want everything America makes, even our junk.

        Even the stubborn Israelis seemed happy. They were actually accepting the idea of peace. Oh, maybe the older ones didn't accept it - - the ones who had been around long enough to see war or hear stories from their parents about all the wars they had with the Arabs. They were the diehards, the last of their kind, but the newer generation welcomed peace. They were sick of war; they were sick of the draft. In fact, there were demands already to get rid of the draft, but the hard-liners and the older Israelis would not give in to that. This was one thing they would not allow yet - - the end of the draft. They had the idea that they always had to be ready to fight. Something like the old Pearl Harbor complex we used to have but we finally got over that. In time they will get over their complex also.

Peace and security were here and everything was fine. The President's approval ratings were high and everything was going even better than he anticipated.

There were, of course, those religious fanatics bringing up all these crazy ideas. Where they got them, the President couldn't understand. They were saying, just by the fact that there was a seven year peace treaty, it was bringing on some cataclysmic event or the end of the world, but they have always said stuff like that. In his mind, they were just a bunch of religious fanatics. He grew up in church, learning the Ten Commandments and reciting the golden rule, and he never heard any of this stuff they kept repeating. They were quoting all these veiled threats from passages in the books of Revelation and Daniel. Everybody knew these were symbolic and not to be taken as real. It was the idea of good versus evil, and the idea that good would triumph over evil someday. Most of the main stream Christians had accepted that idea. It was only the fanatics; the holy rollers who just couldn't let it go. They just couldn't stand the idea that mankind could make peace among themselves, they said, without God. But who is to say God didn't have a hand in this? After all, it is God's desire that man have peace. Who's to say he wasn't behind this?

The status of peace in the Middle East was one of the big items on the agenda for his meeting; the other was this regime in Africa we were supporting. The Republic of Ashanti was a West African country in which the U.S. had a large commitment.

Several years ago the remarkable discovery of huge volumes of oil were made in this country. The leaders secretly asked for and received our help in ascertaining the extent of their oil reserves. We secretly sent our best scientists and used all our best technology on the ground, in the air and from satellites. The unbelievable find was that this country had more oil reserves than the entire Middle East combined. Deals were made, papers signed, and before the rest of the world could jump in, we had locked up the most favorable deal imaginable on oil prices and supply. Because they had something we wanted, we poured in foreign aid, money and weapons to this country. It looked good that we were supporting a developing democracy, but the bottom line came down to this: they had something we wanted.

Now the oil fields were brimming with wells, and the oil was flowing. There were no oil shortages; the monopoly of OPEC was broken. The resulting low oil prices fueled economic development and ended the lingering recession in the United States. There was peace and prosperity everywhere. It was like boom times, and everyone was happy.

To keep Ashanti in our camp and protect our oil interests, the U.S. supplied weapons to their military. Not the kind of second rate weapons usually sent to foreign countries, but our best weapons. We usually sent weapons that are no longer first line, or weapons with some type of capability missing. But, we sent them our best weapons that had basically the same capability as our armament. There was some concern in the military with this. They were afraid someday that we might have to face our own weapons. But it was a decision the President made because he had confidence in our military. He felt nobody could use our weapons as good as us. He felt they were no threat to us, if nothing else because they were all the way across the ocean in Africa. And, if we ever found out they were giving them to a potential enemy we could take them out easily from the air. In fact, we could take out the whole country if needed. But, the whole idea, of that happening, was so farfetched it wasn't a major consideration. The overwhelming factor was good will and continued access to the oil.

There was a buzz on his intercom.

"Yes."

"Mr. President, Gen. Hartsfield and Sec. Adams are here."

"Ok send them in."

He looked at his watch. They were right on time. Looks like I'll get my golf time in today after all.

The creature had swum most of the night down the river past the busy harbor and into the sea. He never fully submerged in the river until he got to the harbor. He submerged there because there were too many boats and people around for him to take a chance on being seen. Now that he was in the ocean he liked the feeling of being totally engulfed by the water.

He was completely exhausted from his trip. He didn't fully understand why, but without the sun he was not getting any energy. That meant when he was underwater or it was night, he was burning his reserve energy. At these times he needed to eat to generate power.

He found he was ideally suited to hunt in the oceans. He had the speed to match or exceed any marine animal. He had the hearing and underwater smell that a shark would envy. He had sensors that could detect movement dozens of miles away and even tell if the objects were alive or not alive. He began to eat hungrily and furiously every marine animal he encountered. He found he had nothing to fear. Even when the predators like sharks and killer whales fought back in desperation their sharp teeth could not penetrate his scales. The animals he ate couldn't provide him with energy as efficiently as the sun. So, he found he had to eat almost continually to keep up his strength. As a result, when he passed through on area he ate everything and left it devoid of major animal life. He left a wasteland in his wake, except maybe for jellyfish and crustaceans out of sight at the bottom. Anything he detected swimming he attacked and ate it.

His keen hunting senses took him through the rich fishing fields off the coast and led him in an easterly direction toward Africa. He was back up to full strength by now, but compulsively continued to kill everything around him. He was like a bear that had gorged himself on salmon during their annual run. Like the bears, he had no need for food at this point. He didn't eat them anymore, but continued to kill just for the sake of killing.

More memory from the little man began to surface in his mind. There was a country in the place called Africa, which was closely aligned with the little man's country. It also has some of the best weapons these humans possess having acquired them from the United States or U.S. as it is also called. What better way to start his mission than to show the humans their best weapons can't stop him? In this country, oil was the thing that was most valued. The creature adjusted his course and headed for Ashanti. Now it knew how it wanted to bring the humans under submission and this country would be its first stop.

CHAPTER 6

Near the end of the first quarter of the 21th century, man had made huge strides in battery technology. Batteries had been developed that were so efficient, small and light weight, that it became practical to send small probes out to sea for months at a time. They require no servicing or recharging during their tour on station. They have the appearance of small torpedoes but are approximately half the size. They are filled with sensors, cameras and GPS technology. They send back all sorts of data on the oceans and can be controlled remotely from thousands of miles away. The camera images are automatically digitally enhanced to remove the clouding effects of seawater. As a result the images are so clear the marine life appear to be swimming in air instead of water, as long as they are in a mile or two of the camera.

Jim Eppley, section chief in the National Oceanographic Survey Administration (NOSA), was reading fishing reports and marine observations from the South Atlantic probes. He began to frown as he read them. The reports seemed to show something unusual. He picked up his phone and called Phil Kona, his senior technician.

"Phil, these reports you sent me, the South Atlantic Ocean conditions for last week, there're all wrong."

"What do you mean?"

"The part that gives me the health of the ocean and the marine life numbers, the data is incomplete or partially missing."

"Oh yeah, I noticed that too. I asked for another report and it came back the same. I got on the horn with Frank Cisco. He rechecked what came in from the probes and the unverified reports from ships at sea. He said the data was correct."

"Well I don't care what they said, these are all wrong. Let me finish looking at this and I'll get back with you."

He began to read and study the data that was sent to him. Almost everything about the South Atlantic sector seemed normal for this time of year. Most of it the marine numbers and variety of life seemed normal. But, there was this huge swath of ocean that seemed almost empty of sea life. There were still tiny minnow sized fish and tons of jellyfish there. But, strangely there were no reports of anything else. Even the normally rich fishing area off the South American coast had the same thing happen there. Also, there were these reports that had been filtered to him from fishing boats and ships at sea. There were numerous reports of all sorts of dead fish and mammals floating to the surface with teeth marks and cut in half. Many were mutilated beyond recognition. Even whales and large sharks were reported dead and floating in the water. These weren't observations from scientists or trained observers but seamen on ships. But there were too many reports describing the same thing to ignore them. What was going on?

The ocean temps were normal. Oxygen content was normal. There was no red tide. Wait a minute. He picked up a pencil and hurried to the map on his wall. He made a mark where the weird data and reports were closest to the South American coast. He made a second mark where the farthest were reported. He went back to his desk and brought the reports back to the map. Then he began to make a mark on the map in the general location of each report. He starred at the points then went over to his phone.

"Phil, I have a job for you. I need this done today, as soon as possible."

"Jim, everybody is busy. I don't have anyone free today."

"Phil, come into my office. I have something to show you."

A few minutes later, Phil walked in and came over to Jim who was still standing at the map.

"Phil, take a look at these points. They are the points were we got the crazy data and info last week."

He took the pencil and drew a line connecting all the marks. When he finished, he had a line that snaked over the ocean.

"I want you to put your best guy on this. The first mark is info from our remote stationary probe off the coast. The rest are GPS locations of probes and visual sightings. I want him to take in account the currents and anything else that would affect something moving through this area. What I want him to do is come up with a general idea where this effect is heading."

"Like I told you everybody is busy."

"Phil, I want you to take your best guy that is good at plotting a course, tell him to drop everything else and work on this. As soon as he is finished bring me the info."

"Ok, you got it."

Two hours later, Jim was looking at a chart of the South Atlantic Phil had brought with him. A black straight line was drawn across the ocean spanning from the coast of South America and ending at a point mid ocean. At the end of the line it changed from black to red.

"I think I know what this is saying but I want to be sure. Tell me what I'm looking at Phil."

"Well what we have here is all the readings and sightings we have on this phenomenon plotted by latitude and longitude. Then we factored in drift, currents, storms and anything else that would affect where these data points were observed vs. where they actually occurred."

Jim interrupted, "so you then wind up with the actual points of occurrence instead of the points where they were seen."

"Yea, that's right. When we finished we came up with pretty much a straight line."

"What's this red line at the end?"

Phil took a deep breath and sighed. "With the conditions that we currently see in front of it, the red line shows what we think is the probable direction this phenomenon will take for the next 48 hours."

"You don't seem too happy with your prediction."

"Well I'm not. We're not in the business of predicting where something in the ocean will move like this. I wouldn't bet on this being accurate. But I will say it's the best guess we could come up with the info we have now."

"Well I have more confidence in you guys than with any group I have ever worked." Jim lifted up his hand and pointed to a spot on the red line.

"Phil, what's the nearest probe we have to this position."

"I think that's about where msp-8 is located. But it's about 100 miles to the southeast."

"I want you to figure out an intercept course and sent it out in front to meet it."

"Send it to meet what?"

"I don't know myself, just do it."

"Even at top speed I don't know if it can be done. You know it's probably going to just about kill the batteries. They're not designed for running at full power for that long."

"I don't care if it kills the batteries. I want to know what's out there."

"Oh yeah, by the way number eight is the problem probe. We've been having problems with glitches in the sensors and cameras for its whole deployment."

"Great, please, just do it and do it as fast as you can."

"Ok Jim."

Phil turned and left the office while Jim continued to stare at the red line on the chart. He was brooding over it and had a bad feeling about this. Something was going on that he couldn't explain and had never before seen. Whatever it was it just couldn't be anything good.

General Jasiri was sitting in front of his TV watching the Satellite News Network (SNN). He was cozy in his oversized recliner watching his favorite channel. He was a news junkie and always enjoyed watching what was happening in the world. But his enjoyment was somewhat tempered because now he watched with a purpose. As Supreme Commander of all the Ashanti defense forces, he was keenly aware of the lack of respect his forces got from the rest of the world. This lack of respect came not so much from his fellow African countries, but from the Western countries, the European bloc, and the new Russian, Chinese and North Korean, Eastern bloc. He was always watching the news looking for any signs of their feelings toward his military. He had attended West Point and spent plenty of time in the United States.

He was keenly aware of the American attitude toward Africa. They smiled and were pleasant toward us. But he felt deep down inside that they don't believe we are equal to them. They sold us all these weapons, but they really don't believe we can use them properly. As a result when his government made the huge deal to get all these advanced weapons he began to train his men hard in their use. He put them through intensive, repeated training. Anyone who showed any signs that they didn't understand how to do their jobs to his standards repeated their training or was washed out.

Many of his commanders complained that he was being too hard. They said he was expecting too much from the men. Many of the men they said, only four years earlier had been herding their father's goats, but he was insistent. He had this windfall of first class weapons in his hands and he was going to have his military fully capable of using them. If not, he would rather not have the weapons at all. He had his subordinates hand pick people who would handle the advanced weapons. Only candidates who proved to their satisfaction that they had the proper aptitude and skills to handle the modern jets, smart munitions and other equipment were even allowed to touch them. Most of his military handled the more traditional hardware. A smaller group of elite soldiers, sailors and airmen in each service became the equal of any military in the world with hi tech weapons.

It just frustrated him to no end that the Western and Block countries didn't respect what his men had accomplished, but he was more upset for his men than himself. Well, if they ever made a move on this country they will pay an unacceptable price, more than they could imagine, he thought. We may not be able to win a conflict with a big power because of our small numbers. But we could surely decimate any first wave sent against us.

Some would say for what purpose was all this necessary? In our short history Ashanti has never fought a war with another country. We have no real enemies as far as other countries are concerned. In fact it could be argued that our various tribes have in the past fought each other more than anyone else. However, the final answer comes back to the oil. Everything came back to the oil. When you are weak and have an asset as valuable as this many envious eyes are watching you. It wouldn't take long before someone decided it's worth the bold step of taking what you have from you and the devil with the consequences.

From the connecting room, a female voice beckoned him.

"Don't you think it's about time you cut off that TV and came to bed?"

He smiled and forgot about all his serious thoughts. His mind went back to a time 30 years ago. He was a young student playing in his school's marching band. They performed at rugby and football games. He was so ambitious; he had his whole future planned out. But there was this young girl named Hasina who worried him to no end. She was definitely not in his plans. She was a flag bearer on the squad and had this huge crush on him. He looked on her as a friend and a nice girl, but she just wasn't his type. He had made in his mind the big mistake of taking her to a formal dance. After that he couldn't seem to get rid of her.

The real true love of his life was the beautiful Sauda. She was perfect in every way. He could still see her now in the blue sequin majorette outfit that she wore that day. She had lovely, dark, perfect skin, beautiful high cheekbones, and a smile that went straight to the deepest part of his heart. Not only that, she was the daughter of the Minister of the Interior. Marrying her would help his career. He hadn't won her yet, so far all his advances were only met with an amused smile from her. But, he could tell she was interested. Whenever he was near her he would catch her quickly turning her head away when he looked in her direction. She was interested all right, but trying her hardest not to let him know it. She was going to be his, it was just a matter of time and him playing his cards right.

However, this Hasina was an unwelcome interference with his plans. She came up to him that day at the field before the band's performance. She began to stare into his eyes with that blissful smile she always gave him. Hasina started babbling on about them as if they were a couple.

"What are you talking about?" he said to her.

"You know since we are in love with each other," but before she could finish her sentence he cut her off.

"I am not in love with you, don't you get it. The person I want is that girl over there." He pointed at the lovely Sauda who was walking over to the bleachers.

"Well, I thought since we made love that night when we went to the dance we were both in love with each other."

"What are you talking about? We never made love. I never tried anything like that with you. Wait a minute; you mean when I kissed you on the forehead?"

"Yes, that's when I knew you loved me - - when you thought too much of me to try to force me to have sex with you. That was the greatest gift anyone could ever give me."

"Don't you get it? I don't want you. I want Sauda. I don't want to kiss or hold you, I want to kiss and hold her."

The smile went away from her face. Her eyes then began to fill with tears. Good, she's finally beginning to understand.

"We are not even of the same tribe. She and I are of the same tribe. Her father is the Minister of the Interior, if I marry her I can get ahead. If I marry out of my tribe, I will displease my parents and I will not get far in this life."

Her body crumbled to the ground. She let herself go and began crying hysterically.

Well, at least she finally understood and can stop this fantasy she has about us, he thought.

But, then, he began to feel so sorry for her. Her reaction stunned and distressed him.

"Hasina, get up its ok. Everything is going to be all right. It's not the end of the world."

He tried to help her up from the ground but to no avail. Her body had gone completely limp. Out of the corner of his eye he saw a fast approaching figure. It was the drum major coming over to see what was wrong and he was irritated.

"What is wrong with you girl? We are about to start in a few minutes."

She kept on crying and didn't answer. Jasiri tried to cover for her.

"She's alright; she just is not feeling very well right now. She had some bad news."

The drum major ignored him and kept yelling at her.

"Well whatever your problem is you better get yourself together. We're starting in a few minutes."

He turned and walked away. For some reason Jasiri didn't like the way the drum major talked to her, he didn't like it at all. He reached down and picked her up. She raised her head and he looked deep into her eyes. Her eyes were red and her face tear stained. He wanted to hold and comfort her, but if he did that she might take it wrong and start that fantasy all over again. Then something remarkable happened; he began to feel a tear swelling up in the corner of his eye. What was happening? It grew larger by the second despite his attempts to stop it. He had to get away before she saw it. He turned and began to step away, to get distance between them. For some reason, his feet didn't seem to work right and he had trouble walking. He forced himself, by sheer will, to put one foot in front of the other and escape. He kept putting one foot in front of the other until he had walked out of the stadium. He kept on walking until he looked up and realized he was downtown and hadn't even noticed he had left the stadium.

What had happened? Could I be in love with Hasina? Then it hit him. He was actually in love with her. In addition, he deeply cared about how she felt and what she thought.

"Are you coming to bed now?" His wife was calling him once again. "Yes Hasina, I'll be there in a minute."

CHAPTER 7

At the office of Jim Eppley, section chief in NOSA, the phone rang. It was Phil Kona on the line.

"Jim, number eight is almost in position. It's going to be close but it looks like we may get a look at whatever it is as it passes in range of the probe. It should be at its closest point in the next fifteen minutes."

"I'll be right over."

Jim jumped up from his desk to head out the door. As an afterthought he picked up a pad and pen and took it with him. He rushed out the door and down the hallway. He opened the door to the small probe control room and entered. This was where the probes were controlled and monitored. There were rows of TV monitors in the room where live raw data was displayed. Usually the feeds were recorded for later analysis, and then put in the form of a printed report. But today was different; they were going to try to make sense out of a live feed as it was happening.

Jim looked around the room. It was crowded with people. It seems like the word got out something unusual was happening, he thought. Most of them were analysts or technicians who worked somewhere else in the section. I should clear them all out except the people who belong here. However I don't blame them; I would want to see this myself.

Phil walked over to him from one of the monitors. "Kind of crowded huh, you want me to clear the room?"

"Nah, leave them alone. How long is it until show time?"

"About ten minutes now. Come on over with me to the control console for number eight."

Phil walked him over to a small row of consoles. There were five consoles with numerous monitors on each one. There was a different display on each monitor showing different types of data. Each console had a set of joysticks that controlled the probes in real time. They controlled things like speed, direction and depth. There were buttons on the joysticks that also controlled the various cameras and sensors. Since the probes were run on automatic most of the time these five consoles were all that were needed for the dozen ocean roaming probes currently at sea. There was a knob on each console that could switch control to any probe, so any console could control any probe. Since the only probe being controlled real time was number eight only one console was manned.

"Since you know how everything works I'm going to wave the usual tour," said Phil. Jim looked up at the large flat monitor on the wall. It was displaying a large underwater image of fish and water. Everything looked normal.

"Oh yeah, when I saw how many people were showing up I piped the feed from the turret cameras to the big monitor. I figured it would give the people here something to look at so they would stay out of the way and out of our hair."

"What's the status of number eight?"

"Just like I thought; the batteries are almost dead. I'm surprised they're still working. We had to cut off everything to save power. We just cut the main camera and the sonar on twenty minutes ago. We left everything else off to save what power we have left. We're using minimum propulsion and are just holding position. We think we're pretty much in the path of the abnormality."

"Pretty much, is that the best we can do?"

"Yeah, I don't guarantee anything. Everything about this is an educated guess."

"Ok, you guys did the best you could and I appreciate it."

"By the way, when we cut the main camera back on one of the glitches showed up. The lens won't zoom. Its set pretty much for a normal view but forget about zooming in on anything. Also, the sonar is working but it will not give an idea of the size or shape of anything, just the speed and direction.

"So in other words you are telling me, we can tell something is out there and if we are lucky enough to get close we may see something."

"Yeah, that is if it's big enough to register on sonar and can be seen visually."

Their conversation was cut short by loud beeps from the console. Dots were racing across the monitor that displayed the sonar feed.

"What's that?" said Jim.

"Something is heading toward number eight, a lot of something. What do you think Frank?"

Frank Cisco was manning the console and operating the systems for number eight.

"Looks like a lot of objects, probably fish swimming our way. I couldn't tell you why." Just as soon as he finished his sentence all sorts of fish and marine animals filled the screen.

"Look at that," said Jim. "It looks like a panicked stampede. I see everything swimming past, sharks, fish, barracudas, predators and non-predators alike. All of them look like they are swimming together in flight, not like anyone is feeding."

"Yeah, that's kind of odd," said Phil.

"Why aren't we picking up anything farther out, behind all this mess?"

"Well, the range is limited on the sonar, a combination of low battery power and one of the glitches."

"Woo," said Frank. I pick up an object on sonar moving fast but not in a straight line. It's moving up, down and darting around, like its attacking."

"What is it?" said Jim, "and what's its size?"

"I can't tell. Everything is showing the same size. I can't tell you anything other than that."

"See if you can get a picture of it with the camera," said Jim.

"I'll try but this thing is moving so fast and erratic it's going to be hard. It won't stand still."

Suddenly the mysterious dot made a swift downward plunge and rapidly accelerated. "I would give anything for a wide angle shot," said Frank.

"Stay with it Frank," said Phil.

Frank was rotating and angling the camera while simultaneously moving and changing the direction of the probe. The dot again changed direction and made a run past the probe.

He struggled to try to get the camera aimed at the target. There was a quick dark flash across the screen and then nothing but water. No fish or anything was on the screen, just water. Then the screen went blank with nothing but static.

"Well the batteries went dead. That's it."

"What about the low power sensors?" said Jim. "Do we have enough power to get any data from them?"

"Naw," said Frank, "the show is over. It should automatically come to the surface and the emergency transmitter should guide our ships to pick it up."

"Did we get anything on the camera? I thought I saw something," said Jim. "Play back that flash near the end."

Frank reversed the recording of the camera feed, and then played it.

"What was that, the blur near the end?" said Jim.

"I don't know," said Frank.

"Reverse it and freeze the picture."

Frank obediently reversed the recording, advanced to the image and froze it.

"It's out of focus, but it looks like a snake, eel or some kind of tentacle," said Jim.

"Yeah," said Phil, "or some kind of a tail."

"There aren't any ocean going animals with a tail shaped like that Phil."

"You're right that's a crazy thought."

"Something is still not right about this picture. How close were we to it? I thought you said we couldn't get close. It looks too big," commented Jim.

"I can't tell how close we were to it. What do you think Frank?"

"Oh, I would say we were about a quarter mile away when it passed by the probe."

"That can't be right," said Jim. "If that's true, how can the image be so large on the screen? Frank, send the recording to the lab and see if they can computer enhance it and get it back to me ASAP."

"OK boss."

Jim looked down at his hand. He was still

clinching the note pad. In all the excitement, he hadn't taken a single note. He took a close look at the image frozen on the screen.

"What is that?" he asked.

Two hours later Jim and Phil were staring at an image on the computer screen from the enhanced video disk.

"What do you think Phil?"

"It's a tail alright, but of what I couldn't tell you. We weren't fast enough to get an image of the body. I guess the thought wasn't so crazy after all."

"Yeah, I agree it's a tail but I can't think of anything in the ocean with a tail like that. It's defiantly not a fish or ocean mammal. What could it be? And there is still something wrong with the size of the image. Frank said this was taken from a quarter of a mile away, right?"

"Well about that, more or less."

"And the lens wasn't zoomed because the zoom wasn't working?"

"That's right."

"Then how come the image looks so large? If the distance is correct the rest of this thing would have to be huge."

"Yeah, I would guess in the ball park with a blue whale."

"Phil that's impossible. Also this tail, it looks like something on a land animal."

"Maybe we're looking in the wrong place, or should I say the wrong time."

"I think I know where you're going and I don't like it."

"Well if there's nothing like this in existence today, maybe we need to look at extinct animals."

"Oh boy, do you know how crazy I am going to sound if I send out a report saying there's a prehistoric animal running loose in the ocean. I might be committed."

"Well who said it was limited to the ocean. Judging by the shape of the tail it doesn't seem to be any good for swimming. I would guess it's an amphibian type that can live on both land and ocean."

Both men starred at each other for a long moment and both sunk in the implication of that revelation.

"Phil I think we're going to need some help on this thing. I want you to send a copy of this to Dr. Drumhill at the Ocean Research Center. We've worked with him before; he's an expert on extinct and prehistoric animals. Make sure you include the data we have on the fish kills with the recording. Send it by the fastest possible means, I'm going to call him and tell him it's on the way. I'm not going to stick my head out to be chopped off without some expert analysis. But, we better get it quick; this thing seems to be heading toward land. If it keeps on its' present course then its' headed toward the West Coast of Africa."

Several days later Jim Apply was at his desk looking over reports when his phone rang. It was Dr. Drumhill at the Ocean Research Center.

"Hello Dr. Drumhill, I'm glad to hear from you."

"Jim, I'm surprised at you. Don't you people have something more important to do than play games?"

"I don't know what you mean Dr. Drumhill."

"Oh, you know what I mean. You almost had me fooled with that clip you sent me. It looked so genuine. But, the more I looked at it I began to see it was a fake."

"I assure you, Dr., what I sent you is real."

"Do you think me a fool Jim? There are no

animals with a tail like that, not swimming in the sea or on land. And I looked at data bases that showed me every known prehistoric animal. There is nothing we know that ever existed with a tail like the one you had on your recording. Also, the animal would have to be gigantic if this recording was taken at the distance you claim."

"Dr., I assure you I am not playing games with you. We came to some of the same conclusions. I need your opinion before I risk going higher with this information."

"You're saying this is real?"

"I most certainly am saying this is real, I wish it wasn't."

"Well, if this is real what you have is almost unthinkable."

"What do you mean by unthinkable?"

"In my opinion you only have two possibilities. One, this is some type of previously unknown prehistoric animal that survived all this time and never went extinct. I consider this highly unlikely."

"Why do you consider that notion unlikely, Dr.?"

"Well, for one thing it's so large; I would guess at least the size of the largest whale. Then, to survive there would have had to be enough of them to mate and produce enough offspring to make up for infant death, accidents or disease. So, unless it's the last one that means there are at least two or three of them. Also, the fact that you took those pictures at such a shallow depth, around 100 feet, makes it even more unlikely they could evade detection all this time. After all, the only reason we never saw a live giant squid in the ocean for such a long time was they swam at great depths. Compared to a giant squid, this thing is practically swimming on the surface. It is highly unlikely with such an enormous size its kind has never been seen."

"And Dr. what is the second possibility?"

"The second possibility I see has an even bigger problem than the first. The tail which I watched over and over again fits no known category. Now taking into account I have only seen the tail, I had to extrapolate what the rest of the animal might be like from this one part. The tail appears to be that of a very large land animal. A tail like that is useless for swimming, but the animal moves at a rapid pace through the water. That tells me it probably has some type of webbing on its feet similar to a duck or a beaver. I noticed the tail seems to be covered with scales. I think they are armored scales for protection similar to that of a prehistoric triceratops or an alligator. But these scales appear to be different, much more sophisticated. I would bet his whole body is covered with them. He probably eats meat and has sharp teeth for ripping and killing. There is a possibility that this animal is amphibious and can operate both on land and water. I think there are other things about it that will greatly surprise us."

"Why do you say that, Dr.?"

"Because there is the distinct possibility this is an unnatural creation which defies all the natural laws of nature. My guess is he is a combination of characteristics that may mimic different animals but could not exist together if naturally evolved."

"You're confusing me Dr., what are you saying?"

"I'm saying the second possibility concludes this thing is probably impossible to exist naturally and had to be created artificially by means unknown."

"But Dr., it's impossible for anyone to create life. We just don't know how to do that, thank God."

"Yes I know, so where does that leave us? I can't think of any other possibilities other than these two. I'm sorry but that's all I can deduct from the information you have given me. Oh, there is one more thing. That data that you sent with the image, about the sea life dying, is it accurate?"

"I would say yes as accurate as we could gather. Well, maybe it's not 100 percent accurate; a large part of it is unverified eyewitness reports from ships at sea. I would categorize it as 75 percent accurate."

"Then we all have another problem, especially if you think the animal is causing this. Is that what you are saying, the animal is causing these fish kills?"

"Yes, Dr. the animal seems to be the cause of the kills."

"Well I ran some computer models on the fish kills. If they continue at the current rate combined with the current poor health of the oceans, the models say in less than 7 years all the fish we consider food will be gone."

"What, are you saying all of the fish will be gone?"

"Oh, not all of them, there will still be fish but just the kind we consider not good for eating. The kind we use in fertilizer and chemicals will still be around. In fact some of the models say this will happen in as little as 5 years, then a few years latter just about nothing will be alive in the oceans. Of course all this depends on the kills continuing at the current rate."

"Thank you Dr. for your input. I don't think I need to ask you not to disclose this information."

"You don't have to worry about that Jim. I'm not going to go out with theories like this and no proof. I gave you my opinion because you asked for it.

What you do with it is your business, but I'm certainly not going to talk to anyone about this."

"Goodbye Dr."

"Goodbye Jim."

Eppley sat back in his chair and thought over the conversation he had with Dr. Drumhill. This information was fantastic and unbelievable. Only a week ago his world was normal and predictable, now everything was turned upside down. What in the world was he to do now? If he opened up this can of worms and he was wrong it could be the end of his career. But if he is right something has to be done to stop this thing now. The sooner action is taken the better it will be for the world. He also thinks he may know how to track its movement. He picked up his phone and called his department director in the NOSA. He has to tell someone about this development.

CHAPTER 8

The sun rose to reveal a cloudy and overcast day in Ashanti. Every now and then the sun would peek through the clouds hinting there was a chance of clearer weather later. It was Foundation Day, a national holiday. On this day the country was officially founded and government offices were closed. Most of the armed forces were also on leave, but Captain Amiri and his patrol boat, the Haraka Meli was still off the coast cruising back and forth. His boat and two others had the dubious task of staying at sea while the rest of the navy was enjoying themselves at home. His craft was a patrol boat similar to patrol boats used by the U.S. Coast Guard but larger. Besides having guns these boats also had sonar detection and anti-ship missile capability which the U.S. boats did not possess.

He thought it ridiculous that he and his men were forced to stay out here for nothing. They had long range radar and airplanes flying over the area all the time, he reasoned. Why can't his men have the day off with their families like everyone else?

Since he had to have the boat out he couldn't stay in port, but as Captain he let all non-essential personal on board take leave. They were at sea with a skeleton crew but only for one day, that's the best he could do. In addition for this one day he let all military decorum go out the window. He let most of the men be off duty and let them sleep late in their bunks. The only divisions on duty were the helm, surveillance and engineering. In fact, he was lying in his bunk relaxing himself when his intercom buzzed. He answered it half asleep.

"Captain, I'm picking up a large sonar contact." It was his sonar man Wachree. Odd he thought, but no reason for concern. "It's probably a whale," said the Captain.

"No I don't think so; they don't usually come in this close, especially one this big."

The Captain started to tell him not to worry about it and call him back when he can figure out the identity of the contact. However, Wachree was one of the best sonar men he had ever seen. He trusted him. Also, he noticed there was a worried tone in his voice.

"I'll be right there, keep track of it."

He slowly got up, put on his shoes, pants and shirt. He started to leave his room with his shirt tails out, but thought better of it and tucked them in his pants. I guess I need to set some example for the men even though I don't feel like it.

On his way to sonar he passed several crewmen, none in uniform. Everyone was relaxed and in high spirits with many in different stages of intoxication. It was a party atmosphere all over the boat. Well good for them, he thought. All we are doing out here is chasing whales anyway.

He walked into the small darkened room where all the surveillance equipment was housed. He noticed Wachree was wearing the loudest colored shirt he had ever seen. It looked like one of those Hawaiian shirts with all the wild colors and big flowers all over it. Where did the men get all this stuff? It was like they pulled it out of thin air; he never saw any of this stuff before today. Oh well, he decided to ignore it.

"Okay, what do you see now?"

"It's changed course a little and is heading more to the north on a heading of 080 degrees," said Wachree. "It's heading away from us."

"I don't know if it's worth following. You still think it's not a whale?"

"Yes sir, I'm almost sure it's not a whale it seems too big. But it's not a submarine or metal object either. We don't detect metal or pick up any propeller sounds."

"Well, there's no animal bigger than a whale. It's got to be some kind of sub. Maybe it's got some kind of stealth coating. We're heading south on 179, we're heading away from it. I think we better investigate."

Captain Amiri hit a nearby intercom button.

"Helm this is the Captain, turn around and change course to 075. Increase speed to 15 knots, I'm on my way to the bridge."

The creature was leisurely swimming through the ocean when he noticed a pinging sound coming from his right side. He had heard this sound once before, a couple of weeks ago. Then it was coming from a little object floating in the sea. This time it was coming from an object cruising on the surface. He recognized this object as one of the human vessels. The sound irritated him so he turned away from the ship. But then it changed course and followed him unlike the last time. So, he speeded up in an effort to get away from the sound.

Amiri reached the bridge and contacted Wachree in the surveillance room.

"What's the contact doing now?"

"It's changed course and speed. It's heading is now 089 degrees and its speed went from 2 knots to 15 knots."

"So it's trying to get away from us. Well he can't outrun us; we can easily do 30 knots. Keep me informed of any change in the contacts position. Helm, lay in an intercept course to the contact. I want to get right on top of it."

The creature noticed the ship had changed course and was speeding up toward him. Well no matter, it was like a fly to him. It wasn't worth the energy to get away from it. He had more important things on his mind. He was almost to its first objective, the oil fields of Ashanti. Now was the time to surface and take a look.

"Captain, said Wachree over the intercom. The contact is rising. I think it's coming to the surface."

There was a loud yell from somewhere behind Captain Amiri. "Over there on the port side." Amiri turned and saw a wake of bubbling sea, and in front of it was a sight he couldn't believe he was seeing. It was the huge head of an animal swimming in the ocean. He grabbed his binoculars to get a better view. It was unlike anything he had ever seen. The head looked like some monster out of a horror story. It was evil looking and can't be real. However it must be real, he was watching it with his own eyes.

"Captain," it was his sonar man again. "I show the contact at or just below the surface."

"It's on the surface all right. I'm looking at it right now. It's some kind of an animal."

"An animal, then Captain I advise we don't get too close to it. The return indicates it is at least as large as us, maybe even bigger."

Captain Amiri was a little startled at the thought

66

of an unpredictable and sinister looking animal larger than his vessel. He sprang into action and issued a series of orders.

"Helm, close to 500 meters and stay there. Don't get any closer."

"Radio, get me headquarters right away."

"Sound general quarters, wake up everybody and get them to their stations."

The alarm rang throughout the boat. Groggy half asleep men rose from their bunks. Actually half the men were in their bunks and the other half were playing cards or watching satellite TV. They were moving in slow motion, mumbling and complaining about being called to general quarters on a holiday. When the alarm stopped the Captain turned to his XO, Lieutenant Kafeel.

"What's our status?"

"A few of our stations are manned but most of them haven't reported in yet."

"Haven't reported? Give me that microphone. This is the Captain; this is not a drill or a game. Everybody get to your stations and report now, and I mean now."

At the sound of Captain Amiri's voice there was a sudden flurry of activity throughout the vessel. His voice, especially the tone of it caused the men to rush to their stations. Something was up and it alarmed them.

"Captain, said the XO, stations are reporting in throughout the boat. All combat stations are manned and ready. Almost all of the other stations have reported in also."

"Good that's better. Radio, do you have HQ yet?"

"No sir, nobody is answering."

Back at coastal patrol headquarters everyone

was gone for the holiday except for a 2nd lieutenant who was officer of the day and one NCO. By noon time the lieutenant saw no reason to stay. Nothing was happening, so he left leaving the NCO to stand watch and man the communications. With no one to stand in for him the NCO was answering the call of nature in the head while reading a comic book and listening to the MP3 player plugged in his ears. The frantic calls went unanswered and fell on deaf ears.

"Keep trying to get HQ," said Amiri.

He noticed their position. This thing is headed toward land. In fact it seems to be heading toward the oil port of Majini. There are lots of ships and oil tankers anchored there. Most of them have crews onboard, unless they're ashore enjoying the festivities. It's too dangerous to allow this thing to enter port.

"Radio, have you contacted anyone yet?"

"No Captain, nobody answers at HQ."

"Well, try the emergency frequencies and any others you can use. We have to get somebody in authority. And call the other two boats. Tell them we have some sort of monster on the surface heading toward Port Majini. We're following him and request help."

Captain Amiri thought over his options. He was out of contact with higher authorities. This thing had made no threatening move toward him so it didn't show hostility. However, he couldn't take the chance of letting something this huge and potentially dangerous enter a harbor full of ships and people.

"Captain, the other boats refuse to come. They say we have had too much to drink and we better get off the radio before we get into trouble."

"The idiots, well I guess I can't blame them. I wouldn't believe a transmission like that myself. Well

I guess it's going to be up to us. XO are all weapons manned and ready?"

"Yes sir."

Amiri just realized he may have to try to kill something he can't even prove existed. In addition, maybe he was about to destroy all the evidence.

"XO send somebody up here with a camera and start taking pictures of this thing."

"Yes sir"

Amiri grabbed the microphone.

"Men this is the Captain, our objective is to turn this thing away from land. Then if we fail that, kill it. If every man does his job as you have been trained, we should have no problem."

He hung up his microphone and turned to his helmsman.

"Give me twenty knots. Keeping our same distance steer a course around this thing and take a position in front of it. Keep the boat perpendicular to its course; do not get directly in its path."

The crew and ship responded to his commands. The vessel speeded up, passed the creature and took a position ahead of it, but 90 degrees alongside its path. They then slowed down to match the animal's forward motion. The creature watched them with contempt but was not going to react to any action from them. Why should he react to flies?

Amiri keyed his microphone, ".50 Cal guns, at my command start firing across his path into the water. Start 100 meters in front of it then bring the fire gradually toward him. I want you to stop at 20 meters in front of it. Do not, I repeat, do not hit it."

Captain Amiri watched and waited until the animal was in the position he wanted, and then gave the command, "Open fire."

The dual .50 Cal machine guns mounted forward and aft opened up. Tracers hit the water spitting foam and water into the air. The columns of water raced across the ocean and stopped in front of the huge head. Then there was quietness. There was no response from the creature, it just kept swimming in the same direction.

"Helm, keep our position in relation to the animal the same regardless of its movement. Now get us back in position; we're going to try it again. Where is that camera? Are we getting any pictures of this?"

The XO responded, "Our camera man is on leave for the holiday, but one of the crew men is on deck with his cell phone taking pictures."

"Just great, the only record of this whole thing is going to be on a cell phone."

Amiri and his crew swiftly moved into position again and repeated the same maneuver. Again .50 Cal tracers sent up plumes of water into the air stopping 20 meters short of the animal. There were no results, it kept going on the same course and didn't change direction.

"Captain," said the XO we're within sight of land. I make it four kilometers to Port Majini."

"Well that's it. Send out this message on all military channels, Navy, Air Force, Army or anyone that can receive it. Attempts to turn animal away from land were unsuccessful. It appears to be heading to Port Majini. On Captain's initiative I'm going to attack the animal with the intent to kill it."

CHAPTER 9

Colonel Fahamu, commander of the 437Th Tactical Air Wing of the Ashanti Air Force, was eating in the almost empty officer's mess when his cell phone rang. He looked at the caller ID and saw it was a lieutenant in his HQ who was on duty today.

"Sir, I hate to bother you but we've been picking up a number of strange transmissions from navy patrols off the coast. I wouldn't have bothered you but I think you should know about these crazy messages."

"Well what are they?"

"Sir, one of the ships claims it's fighting some type of monster."

"What kind of crazy nonsense is this? Is the navy playing some type of game? Are you sure this is a navy transmission?"

"Radio direction shows us the signals are coming from off the coast at the approximate location they say they're located. But it seems like the other ships out there don't believe him and refuse to come help him."

"What's the name of this ship of lunatics?"

"It says it's the Haraka Meli."

"The Haraka Meli, that's Captain Amiri's patrol boat."

Colonel Fahamu knew Amiri well. He was a

few years younger than him but they had attended the same high school. They both excelled in their studies and went on to study at the same University. In his mind there is no way Captain Amiri would send out a message like that unless he thought it was true. That means either the message is true or he has fallen for a great hoax. Nevertheless he knows him, Captain Amiri is no fool. That means if this message is from him it's probably true.

"What's his location?"

"He said he is four or five kilometers southwest of Port Majini. He also said the monster is heading for the port and he is trying to stop him."

"Heading for Majini? Do we have anything in the air near that area?"

"We have a C-130 cargo plane on a training flight that's set to pass the port area in about twenty minutes."

"Tell them to forget the training mission and vector them to the area of the last transmission. I want them to go low level and report what they see."

"Yes sir."

The Colonel sat back in his chair suddenly having lost his appetite. If this report was correct it couldn't have happened on a worse day. He picked up his phone and called HQ.

"Are the alert aircraft ready to launch?"

"Sir we have two aircraft ready but we don't have anyone to fly them right now."

"What do you mean?"

"Well the pilots got tired of waiting around with nothing to do so they went back to the barracks."

"What, send the MP's to get them and put them in their cockpits. And, make sure they stay there until I say they can get out."

"Yes sir."

Captain Amiri had maneuvered his boat into a position 300 meters to the rear of the animal. He had at his disposal four .50 Cal machine guns, one 20 mm Gatling gun firing explosive rounds and two ship to ship missiles similar to the Harpoon class missile. However, he had no intention of using his missiles. It would be a waste of money using missiles on an animal.

Amiri was running out of options. They were only four kilometers from the port entrance.

"All .50 Cal's open fire on that thing," said Amiri. The loud bark of heavy machine guns once again filled the air. Tracers reached out just short of the target, then were walked up the water to the intended target. Splashes were all around the gruesome head, so many that sometimes it disappeared among the splashes. Many of the tracers were being deflected up and in all directions.

The ocean is certainly bouncing up a lot of our shots today, thought Amiri. The thing however, never changed course. After a minute or so of constant firing he yelled, "Cease fire."

To his disbelief the thing was still swimming as if nothing had happened.

"Kafeel, with all that firing, why haven't we hit him? What's wrong, are the gunners blind?"

"No sir, I was watching through my binoculars. Most of the rounds were direct hits. They just bounced off him."

"Bounced off him? .50 Cal rounds don't just bounce off an animal. Open fire with the 20mm then."

"Yes, sir."

The XO gave the order and the loud staccato sound of the machine guns was replaced by the deep throaty whine of the 20mm Gatling gun. Explosive cannon rounds flew out of the muzzle at the rate of

6600 rounds per minute. Flashes danced all over the creature's head and the water around him. There could be no question to everyone who was watching he was being hit. The creature's response to this was to continue swimming as if nothing was happening. He just ignored the fire and continued on his way.

"I think we have a serious problem," said Amiri to his XO. "Cease fire."

He thought for a long few seconds while starring at the creature still swimming toward the port. He then turned to the XO.

"Do we have a target lock on that thing with the missiles?"

"Yes sir."

"It's time we end this thing."

"Captain," said the radioman, "the Captain of the Gazelle which is patrolling north of us said he is coming to help. He said he will be here in 20 minutes."

"Tell him thanks but everything will be over before he gets here."

He turned to the XO. "Where on his body is the target lock."

"It's locked on its head; it's the only part of it showing above water."

"Take it off automatic and adjust the impact for a point about two meters behind the head and slightly below the water line. I don't want to take a chance on missing it altogether. The head is probably the smallest part of it."

Too bad, thought Captain Amiri, after being hit with a missile there isn't going to be much left for the scientists to examine. Why do I have to be the one to destroy it?

"Missile ready," said the XO.

"Fire missile."

Colonel Fahamu had returned to his office. His meal was ruined by the reports he had received so he felt he might as well go back to work.

"Colonel Fahamu", said the voice on the intercom.

"Yes."

"We have a report from the C-130. It passed over Port Majini and saw nothing unusual. But, just a few seconds ago they called back and said they saw a missile launch out at sea."

"A missile launch?" His old friend Amiri has really committed himself now. No one cares if he fires a few rounds of cannon shells and bullets into the ocean, but firing one of his expensive missiles is another thing. He's going to have to answer for this.

"Ask them do they see a target? At what are they firing?"

There was a long pause.

"The pilots report they don't see anything. They are too far away. All they see is the smoke from the missile exhaust."

"Well, tell them to go to the area and report back."

"Yes sir."

Back at the patrol boat the crew watched the plume of smoke from the missile as it arched upward in a curving flight to the target. It was designed to hit the target from above. When it reached the highest point in its trajectory it dived downward and hit the creature near the shoulder blades. There was a huge orange, reddish explosion, then smoke that completely obscured the area. The men cheered on the bridge and there were shouts of joy all over the boat.

"Send out a message to the other boats and

HQ," said Amiri. "Direct hit scored on the animal with a missile. We're going over to the scene to pick up any animal parts we can find for examination."

"Captain," said the XO. "You better take a look."

Amiri picked up his binoculars and was startled at what he saw. Through the clearing cloud of the explosion he could see the big ugly head of the animal. It was still there, but now instead of facing away from him it was turned toward him.

The creature had mostly ignored the patrol boat and continued on his way. It heard a noise from somewhere behind him but didn't bother to look. Suddenly he was hit by a tremendous explosion which rocked him and shoved him downward. It didn't really hurt him, but like a boxer in the ring who didn't see a punch coming it knocked a little of the wind out of him. He wasn't braced or prepared for the blow because he didn't see it coming. He turned and examined the small vessel. One of the little pointy objects on the deck was missing, there were two of them but now there was only one. That's what they must have used on me, he thought. Now they were a threat to him and he had to deal with them.

As Captain Amiri examined the creature through his glasses he became aware the animal was also examining them. From deep down inside him he recognized what the animal was thinking. Amiri was a city boy, born and raised in the city. So he was no expert on wild animals. All he really knew about them he learned from watching the nature channels on satellite TV. However, he had spent many summers around farm animals at his grandfather's farm as a youth. Once they had cornered a wild dog that had been killing his grandfather's chickens. Instead of trying to get away it lunged at them and his grandfather barely shot him in the nick of time. Just before he struck out at them he had this same look. It was the look of a cornered animal that was sizing you up just before it was going to attack.

Amiri barked orders.

"XO do we have missile lock on the target with the second missile."

"Not yet, in just a minute."

"Don't do anything fancy this time, just go with auto and fire as soon as you get a lock."

Suddenly the creature dived beneath the water and disappeared.

"Sonar keep track of it," said Amiri.

"It's diving straight down. Now it's coming slightly toward us but still diving," said sonar.

"Now we can't hit him and I think he knows it," said Amiri to his XO.

"What do you mean, he knows it Captain? He's only an animal."

"Oh, you still think he's only an animal? I hope you're right, but there's something that doesn't feel right about this whole situation. Well we're not going to sit here and be a target for him. Change course 90 degrees to port, make speed 18 knots. If it thinks we're going to be sitting in the same spot when he come up he's surely mistaken. Sonar where is he now."

"The return is scattered, I lost him. He must have got below a layer of water with a weird change in temperature or salinity."

"Now we're blind and toothless. Helm, change course 20 degrees starboard. Radio, send this message. Made direct hit on animal with missile, no effect. The animal has dived and I believe we are under attack. I'm taking evasive action."

"Captain," said Wachree, "he has broken out of

the layer and is coming up fast from directly below us."

"Full speed ahead," yelled Amiri, but it was too late.

The massive creature hit the bottom of his boat with the force of a locomotive. The boat partially lifted out of the water. The crew and everything that wasn't tied down flew in all directions. As it settled back down into the water the creature ripped open the bottom of the boat with its massive cruel claws. Seawater began to pour in and it began to sink.

"Radio," yelled Amiri, "call out a mayday, give our position then get out." He turned to his XO, "Call for all hands to abandon ship."

CHAPTER 10

Back at the airbase Colonel Fahamu's intercom buzzed again.

"Yes," he answered.

"Sir the pilots report they see a ship sinking and are picking up emergency signals. It looks like it's the Haraka Meli."

"Do they see any kind of animal in the vicinity?"

"No sir, they only report the Haraka Meli sinking and survivors in the water. But they say the boat's last message said the animal was headed for Port Majini."

"Launch the alert aircraft, tell them to hold station over Majini and report anything unusual. Tell the C-130 to circle as long as they have fuel so they can guide the rescue ships, and tell them to keep radioing the sinking position to anyone who may be nearby."

He thought for a minute and then hit the intercom button for his second in command.

"Call back everyone on leave. I don't care how you do it, but get everyone back to base immediately. Start with the squadron commanders; tell them to call in their flight and ground crews first. Get someone to help you and assign them to call in the higher ups and the pencil pushers. Tell the squadron commanders to fuel and arm their planes for ground attack. If you need any additional help let me know."

"Yes sir, but if they ask what should I tell them they're going to attack?"

Fahamu's lips turned upward into an involuntary but still grim smile. "If they ask tell them it's the bogeyman."

The Colonel reached for his phone. He was about to break protocol and jump the chain of command. It wasn't in his nature to do this but he had a gut feeling they had to respond now or a tragedy of epic proportions was about to occur. He dialed the number for the Commander of the Air Force. The messages said the animal was heading to Port Majini. This was no normal animal. Nothing alive could take a direct hit from a ship to ship missile and survive. If one of those things hit an aircraft carrier in the right spot it could sink it, and this thing sounded almost intelligent. Why was it headed for the one port on which rested our whole economy? He didn't know why but somehow he had the feeling this thing was not limited to the ocean and could operate on land also. That's why he gambled and ordered his aircraft fitted with ordnance for ground attack instead of naval attack. He settled back and loosened his tie while he was waiting for an answer. Today is going to be a long day.

The two F-35 Lightning II alert fighters were circling the port of Majini. Although this fighter had been in active service for almost 15 years now, because of continual upgrades it was still the western world's main choice as their front line fighter. Most countries also continued using the fighter because of the exorbitant price of the latest aircraft with no significant increase in their capability. Their pilot's code names were Tango One and Tango Two.

Tango One was in command of the flight.

"Tango One to Tango Two, do you see anything?"

"I see nothing but a bunch of ships in the harbor. Why are we still circling here?"

"I don't know. Our orders are stay on station and report anything unusual."

After being just about dragged from their bunks by MP's and dressed down by the CO, they had sat in their cockpits for what seemed like hours in the sweltering heat. So they were glad when the call came to scramble their aircraft. Then they could close their canopies and cut on their air conditioning. It also was another chance to get into the air and fly, something all pilots love to do. After circling the same area for fifteen minutes, however, they both were getting bored.

Their two F-35's were lightly armed for both the air and ground role. Since they would be the first to respond and the threat would by necessity be unknown, they carried a mixed bag of ordinance. Tango One was armed with two AIM-132 ASRAAM missiles for attacking enemy aircraft. He was also armed with two 1000 lb. unguided or "dumb" bombs for the ground attack role. Tango Two was armed with two ASRAAM missiles and two CBU-87 cluster bombs. Their weapons were mounted in their two internal weapons bays so they could keep their stealth capability. The two pilots were using their sensors and radar to search for any threat and monitoring the results which were being displayed on their helmet visors. They didn't see anything unusual except a large aircraft curiously circling out over the ocean. Its signature registered it as a C-130, probably the one belonging to their wing. Why it was circling so long over the ocean was anybody's guess.

The creature swam into the entrance of the harbor undetected. No one was looking for him or noticed him. He scanned the area. There were seven or eight oil tankers at anchor. These would be his first victims simply because they were there. He felt himself building up a rage that could not be contained. It was time to destroy and kill. He went to the nearest tanker, dived beneath it and ripped out the bottom. The fuel tanks for its engines were hit and there was a tremendous towering explosion. Circling overhead the F-35's saw the explosion.

"Tango One did you see that?"

"I couldn't help but see that, what happened?"

"I don't know, that tanker suddenly exploded."

"Call it in to HQ and stay with me. Let's go over and take a closer look."

The creature rapidly went from one tanker to another and repeated the same procedure. There was another huge explosion from yet another unfortunate tanker.

"There goes another one," said Tango One. "I don't pick up any missiles or threats on my display do you?"

"No, I don't pick up anything either."

"Well something is doing this. Forget the computer stuff, use your eyes. Look for something visually."

In his lust for destruction the creature put caution more and more to the wind. He surfaced and went between the ships in the harbor. Sometimes when he ripped the ships open they exploded, other times they just took on water and started sinking in the harbor.

"Tango One, I see something in the water at 12 o' clock low. It looks like some kind of animal between two ships."

"Yeah, I see it. I can't believe what I'm seeing.

It looks like its attacking the ships."

Another ship exploded, burning oil began to spread over the water. Men on fire and screaming were diving into the water trying to escape the inferno only to meet more flames on the surface. There was complete chaos in the harbor. Tango One reported what they saw and he listened intently as he received his orders from HQ.

"Tango Two, our orders are to attack and kill the animal as soon as he is in an area free of civilians."

"Well we can't drop ordinance on him in the harbor. There are too many ships and people in the water. And the docks and warehouses are probably loaded with people too."

"Yeah, we're going to have to wait until it leaves the harbor area."

Back at the base there was a flurry of activity as ground crews and pilots began to arrive and quickly organize into teams. They rushed to fuel and arm the planes, but there were too few of them. They were at less than a quarter strength and everything was disorganized.

The creature tired of sinking ships and climbed out of the water at the docks. He turned his attention to the areas were the oil was sent to be loaded on the tankers. He recognized this was a key part of their oil supply network. He ripped into the plumbing, pipelines, valves and warehouses with his paws, claws and the sheer force and weight of his indestructible body. The pilots watched helplessly as he tore apart the oil loading structure of Majini. There was no way they could safely drop their weapons among all the people in the area.

Elisha Washington was a young, bright

83

reporter for SNN in Ashanti. Her friends called her Leesh. Although over time her nickname became so used by everyone, she was never called Elisha but only Leesh. She always wanted to be a journalist and excelled in her studies at school. She impressed the recruiters for the network so much she was hired on the spot by SNN. The recruiters saw raw talent and potential in her and they were not about to pass up on a chance to corral her. They didn't tell her but she was hired not out of need, but mainly to make sure another network didn't get her. The network brass felt she needed more seasoning so they sent here to the far away country of Ashanti. It was peaceful and quite there. It was a place where she could stay out of trouble and still learn the nuts and bolts of the craft. Since there were only a few people staffed there she would have to do several jobs and learn from the ground up how things worked in a newsroom.

Leesh was ecstatic at the opportunity but not too happy when she learned of her assignment. Ashanti, why in the world would I be sent there? Nothing ever happens in Ashanti. However, she quickly put her negative thoughts out of her head. This was her big chance and she was going to make the best out of it. As far as she was concerned she was going to do like the Bible said. Didn't it say if there be anything good dwell on that?

God, church and the Bible meant a lot to Leesh. It was hard for her to leave her church family at Hebron Cornerstone Church and relocate to far off Ashanti. On the other hand she figured God was everywhere, even in Ashanti. Also, there was that strange meeting she had with her Pastor, K.L. Warren that finally made her decide to go. He told her it was her destiny to play a big role in future earth shaking world events. He said he didn't know what they were but she was being put in this situation by God for a reason. She didn't understand what he was talking about, but somewhere deep inside; her spirit was in agreement with what he said.

She worked for the SNN bureau chief in Ashanti, Sam Hobby. Sam was a seasoned veteran journalist who basically had been put out to pasture in the far off country. He was really only there to get his last few years in before he retired. He spent his younger years in the thick of action in all the world's hotspots. He had reported countless wars, genocides, massacres and killings. He was sick of all the turmoil and political upheavals so he was glad to take the post in Ashanti. After they had solved their tribal differences it had become one of the most peaceful and boring places in the world, just the way he liked it. He welcomed the young female journalist. She was eager to learn and willing to do any job. She took a lot of work off his hands and in fact gave him plenty of free time away from the office. Sam liked the young understudy and tried to teach her everything he had learned from working 50 years in the media.

Leesh enjoyed working under Sam's tutoring and was learning a lot. On the down side she was getting bored with the peaceful, uneventful life in the West African country. Other than the occasional domestic violence case, petty robbery or traffic accident, there was nothing to report on in Ashanti except more stories on the oil industry. As a result she had developed a habit of looking for stories that would make a splash. There had to be something out there that would make the network news feed. She would settle for a political scandal, corruption or something that would make the world news. So far she hadn't seen anything, but she was always on the lookout for any signs of a story.

Today she was roaming the crowd at one of the many outdoor Foundation Day events looking for a story. Her boss Sam took the evening off and was at home relaxing, since this was considered a light news day. It was a carefree and joyful atmosphere over the area. The people there were laughing and enjoying themselves. Nothing newsworthy about that, she thought. Oh well, maybe I'm looking too hard. Maybe for once I should just let my hair down and enjoy the day like them.

She walked over to one of the many colorful booths selling food and other items. Leesh began to browse and she found herself involuntarily swaying with the music which seemed to be coming from every direction. The rhythm of the music was catchy, almost hypnotic. However, it was punctuated by the ringing of cell phones in the crowd. Leesh laughed at the thought that no matter where you seem to go there is a cell phone ringing.

Curiously she noticed there was one, then another, then another phone ringing like a chain reaction. The rings had turned into a cascade of sound. They were ringing more and more frequently all over the crowd. She turned and scanned the area. Men and some women were answering their phones then hurriedly leaving. Many of them were in uniform. She noticed the ones that were not in uniform had that military look. She grew up in Virginia Beach, Virginia in an area well known for a large military presence. The look was a combination of their age, the way they cut their hair, the way they dressed and the way they carried themselves that identified military people to her. She also observed it was not just one service that was rushing away. She saw Army, Navy and Air Force members all leaving. Something has to be up.

Leesh reached into her purse and retrieved her cell phone. She called the office where Mark Hammond, one of the editors was left in charge by Sam.

"Mark is there anything happening? I see a lot of military people getting calls and leaving in a hurry."

"Nah, I don't know of anything happening. Maybe they're just having some sort of military exercise."

"No, I don't think so. Why would they do that on their biggest holiday of the year?"

"Well, I'll call around to our usual sources and see if I can find out anything."

"Who's in today?"

"Almost nobody is here, just me, one of the cameramen and oh yeah, the helicopter pilot. He's in here fooling around, probably because he has nothing else to do. I'll call you back as soon as I hear something."

"In the meantime I'm going to see what I can find out here."

Leesh studied the crowd and looked for the nearest military looking person answering one of the curious calls. A short skinny looking young man wearing an army uniform was answering his phone a few feet away. She walked over to him and tried to hear what was being said. She didn't hear anything but his side of the conversation, and all she heard was him saying yeah and ok. She decided it was time for a more direct approach. As he hung up and was beginning to leave she stood in his path and pulled out her press card. Holding it up to him she said, "My name is Elisha Washington with SNN. Sir, can you tell me what is the nature of the apparent military recall that is in progress?"

The young soldier's eyes widened at the sudden appearance of the reporter asking questions. They quickly narrowed however when he looked around and saw no camera recording their conversation. He shook his head no, grunted, stepped aside and walked away, waving her off with his hands. Not one to give up easily Leesh tried the same tactic on at least a half dozen people but basically only got the same result. Her phone rang; it was Mark on the line.

"Leesh, our sources say there was some sort of explosion in Majini, maybe an oil tanker or a storage tank. The local stations are on their way to the scene now."

Leesh was alert; her reporting instincts begin to rise up in her.

"Mark, I think we finally got a real story to report. Can you get the helicopter ready? Give me a cameraman and we can be live in 25 minutes with this story. I know this will make the network."

"Now wait a minute, do you know how much it costs to send out the chopper? I don't think I have the authority to do that anyway. Besides, you are the most junior reporter here. Why should I send you out?"

"Well, look around you; I'm the only reporter you have today. The other two are off hundreds of miles away. And if you are thinking about sending the helicopter to pick them up it would take a few hours round trip just to get them to the story. Come on, we're only 50 miles from Majini."

"What you say makes sense but Sam is going to have to sign off on this. I better call and touch bases with him first."

"Well you better make it fast. The local stations probably are already ahead of us on this story. We better hurry up if we're going to use our own footage on the network broadcast."

Having their own footage was a serious matter to SNN. They prided themselves in using their own camera footage on their news broadcasts. Only when they didn't have their own recorded video or a live broadcast did they ever consider using an outside source. Then they were forced to use the dreaded caption on the bottom of the screen which let the world know the video came from another outlet.

"I'm calling him now. You better get in here as soon as you can."

"I'm in walking distance of the studio. I'll be there in ten minutes. I've been walking toward the studio the whole time."

By the time Leesh had reached the studio Sam had approved her idea. In a few minutes she and a cameraman were in the air to get video of the event.

CHAPTER 11

After venting his anger on the ships and dock areas the creature set his sights on the nearby oil fields. He advanced toward them at a leisurely pace. The edge of the largest was only three or four miles from Majini which made the port so important for oil shipment. It was so close oil was easily sent by pipeline to be shipped at the port. The offshore wind was blowing in a generally easterly direction. As a result the smoke from all the destruction in the port sometimes obscured him visually from the air. However, it was not enough to keep the pilots in the two F-35's circling overhead from getting a good view of him. As he left the harbor area the two pilots saw their chance.

"Tango One to Tango Two, he's in the clear. Arm your weapons. Weapons free, I'm going to attack. This should be easy. I'm going to take him out with my two 1000 pounders. Stay up here and monitor my strike."

"Roger Tango Two."

Tango One rolled his aircraft in toward the target. The grotesque animal was in the clear. The pilot had a good lock on him. Nothing was going to save him now. He had set his drop for salvo so as he pressed his release button both his bombs dropped simultaneously from their bays. As he dropped his bombs the pilot advanced his throttles and accelerated away from the eventual twin blasts.

The creature saw the two fighters circling overhead and noticed they stopped their circling pattern and flew toward him. He knew they were going to attack now. He also knew the puny men put their faith in weapons that were delivered from the air. From what he learned from the Dr's memory jets, missiles and bombs are what they always think will save them when they are in trouble. He watched as the two bombs fell toward him, but stood still so he could be hit. Now it's time for the lessons to begin.

One bomb was a direct hit and impacted him at mid torso. The second one was a near miss and hit the ground only a few feet from his right side.

"Tango One, I saw a direct hit and a near miss almost right on top of him. But believe it or not he's walking away with apparently no injuries."

"What, are you sure I hit him?"

"Yeah, I watched you and you scored a direct hit."

"This is impossible, just the blast from one of them should have killed him. I see him now. I'm in position to observe for you. Use your cluster bombs. Let's see if he can handle them. Give him one on the first pass, if he's still standing after than go around and give him the other."

"Roger, Tango Two going in to the target."

Tango Two carried two cluster bombs. Each contained 202 high explosive bomblets. Each bomblet was designed on explosion to break into approximately 300 fragments that fly outward in all directions. The bomblets are released from the bomb in flight and form a rectangular pattern of explosive death about 200 by 400 meters. It was effective against armored vehicles, artillery or devastating against troops. The pilot of Tango Two held his release until he had the creature firmly within the middle of his pattern area and pressed his release button. The bomb dropped from his aircraft, sailed through the air and released its payload above the animal. The bomblets spilled out of the canister and laid out a perfect pattern. Explosions ignited all around the creature. The air was filled with explosions and deadly shrapnel. Then there was calm and the only sound was that of the two jets.

"Tango Two, this is Tango One; he's still standing. What does it take to kill this thing? Go around and give him your last cluster."

Tango Two came around again and did a second drop. This time it wasn't as perfect as the first but the target was still near the center of his pattern. All the animal did was look up at them and slowly walk away.

"Maybe we didn't get up today and are still in our bunks dreaming all of this because this can't be real," said Tango One. "How's your fuel? I'm close to bingo, just enough to return to base safely."

"I'm already at bingo."

"Let's head home. That's all we can do."

"Don't you want to strafe him on the way out? We still have our guns."

"No, I think it's going to be a waste of time doing that. What we hit him with should be enough to kill anything. A few more rounds from our guns aren't going to make a bit of difference. Close in on me, we're heading back. Now I have to call in this report. Nobody is going to believe me."

Back at the air base the action reports of the two pilots were met with disbelief and confusion. Something was terribly wrong. Either their weapons were not working properly or the pilots were lying.

Over 23,000 miles above the Atlantic Ocean a U.S. intelligence satellite was in orbit. Among other things, it was listening for any type of signal intelligence data or SIGINT of interest. It was scanning an area spanning eastern South America to the Western part of Africa and the area north and south between the poles. SIGINT is a category of intelligence that includes transmissions associated with communications, radars, and weapons systems used by possible adversaries.

It picked up radio communications indicating military activity and explosions in the Port Majini area of Ashanti. All communications were Ashanti military which indicated there was no conflict with outside forces. The information was downloaded to National Security Agency (NSA) computers on the ground. There it was analyzed by programs and categorized as low priority, possibly war games. As low priority the information was not put on any reports or alerts but was recorded and stored for future analysis.

Captain Amiri and his crew had been plucked from the sea by his sister boat the Gazelle. Several men were still unaccounted for so the Gazelle was slowly plying back and forth over the area looking for more survivors. While in the water they had drifted from the sight of land, but as he and his exhausted men lay on the deck he watched huge black plumes of smoke rise from below the horizon to high into the sky. He could tell they were coming from the vicinity of Majini. He also could recognize the distinctive look of burning oil. The port must be under attack by the animal they had fought. The Captain hung his head. Could he have done something differently to prevent all of this? Tears filled his eyes when he thought of all the lives that were being lost and all the destruction that is taking place right now. While all of this is taking place here he sits soaking wet on the deck of a ship unable to help or do anything about it. Something about this scene pricked his memory. It reminded him of Bible verses he once read. It was something about the destruction of Babylon, in Chapter 18 of the Book of Revelation, if he remembered correctly. How did that go he thought? It went something like this:

The merchants of these things, which were made rich by her, shall stand afar off for the fear of her torment, weeping and wailing.

And saying, alas, alas, that great city, that was clothed in fine linen, and purple, and scarlet, and decked with gold, and precious stones, and pearls:

For in one hour so great riches is come to naught. And every shipmaster, and all the company in ships, and sailors, and as many as trade by sea, stood afar off,

And cried when they saw the smoke of her burning, saying, what city is like unto this great city?

And they cast dust on their heads, and cried, weeping and wailing, saying, Alas, alas, that great city wherein were made rich all that had ships in the sea by reason of her costliness: for in one hour she is made desolate.

My God, how in the world can this be happening to us?

General Jasiri was angry when he was first contacted at his home regarding the epic events unfolding in his country. He was not in the mood for games and considered the initial reports some sort of joke or hoax. As more action reports came in however, he had to come to the conclusion something was happening. Of course the wild claims of an animal sinking ships and destroying the wharf areas of a major port couldn't be true. On the other hand he couldn't deny the port was under some sort of attack. As for the nature of the attack, well he still wasn't sure who was attacking them.

When this became evident to him his first thought was not duty, but where is Hasina his wife? She and a friend had gone out shopping and he wanted to make sure she wouldn't blindly stumble into the combat area. As he rushed to his command center the thought came to him he wasn't sure where the combat area was himself. He knew there was chaos in Majini but who knows where this enemy was going to strike next. He was relieved when he finally got Hasina on her phone. He told her to stay put and he sent a helicopter to take her to their vacation home in the mountains. If this does turn out to be some kind of huge animal it will be the safest place he could think of right now. It would be pretty hard for it to climb up that high.

With that matter taken care of, when he reached his command center he turned his full attention to the crisis at hand. He held a conference call with the commanders of the Army, Navy and Air Force. They assured him despite their own initial misgivings it appears both from eyewitness accounts and combat reports the unthinkable was true. A huge monstrous animal is causing a rein of destruction in his country. Also, it looks like he is not finished but has the intention of creating even more destruction. Even worse the military claims numerous direct hits on the animal with no effect.

"How is this possible? We have the latest technology and the best weapons," said Jasiri to his commanders. "How can an animal make a fool out of us? Something else has to be going on here. Some

95

other country has to be involved, but no matter what it is we have enough force to take care of the matter."

General Jasiri had ordered the call up of all his armed forces and was distressed at the slowness of their response. Initial reports showed none of the services at combat strength with numerous units missing so many key personal that they were effectively classified non-operational. He ordered his services to deploy all the units they could to the defense of the country. The Navy was ordered to stand guard off the coast. The Army and Air Force were sent to block and destroy any attack from Majini toward the major oil fields. Reserves were to be held back to respond to any attack from the North, South or Eastern border. Intelligence showed no buildup along the borders, but no buildup or threat was detected prior to this current assault.

When this is over our entire intelligence apparatus is going to have to be looked at and overhauled, he thought. Obviously it has failed us miserably.

A few minutes after ending his conference call an aid rushed into the room.

"Sir, we have live footage from Majini."

The large main screen in the command center switched from a static display of military units and their deployment to a live ground view from one of the local TV channels. The view was horrific. There was a wide angle panning shot of the harbor and warehouse areas on the screen. Fires and huge columns of thick black smoke were rising from the warehouses and from the harbor itself. All the fires were raging out of control with no firefighting taking place. What he didn't see was that the witnesses to the event were so terrified at what they saw there was a complete breakdown of order. The people were so traumatized by the creature's rein of destruction they fled for their lives. All traces of law and order fell and it was every man or woman for themselves. There was no effective policing or firefighting effort in the city.

CHAPTER 12

As the creature reached the outer edge of the main oil field he looked around and pondered his best method of attack. He wanted to destroy it all but he really didn't feel like expending the amount of time and effort it would take to accomplish that. He would have to go to each well and rip out the plumbing and oil transfer apparatus for hundreds of wells. Even then the oil buried underneath the ground would still be there. No he would have to be satisfied with maximum disruption of the oil fields instead of complete destruction.

He hadn't run into any major opposition yet, which surprised him. A few troops had fired at him with their small arms to no effect. He had been hit by a few rounds from a couple of tanks he passed on the way to the fields. The tanks quickly raced away when he turned to respond to their fire, and he didn't feel like chasing them. The creature was intelligent, much more intelligent than man could imagine. He knew who he was and he knew although he looked like an animal he was not really an animal. He looked like flesh and blood but actually he was an imitation of flesh and blood. He was energy that was changed to matter. He also had the ability to change his matter back to energy and to duplicate any damaged or missing body parts. Suddenly he knew what he was going to do.

Meanwhile, the local media was scrambling back and forth trying to get a better shot of what was happening in Majini but they couldn't get any closer than a few miles. The police and military set up crowd and traffic control roadblocks to control the panic and movement at the edges of the city. And they weren't in the mood to entertain the needs of newsmen. Many of the locals who survived the attack told the reporters the huge animal that caused this headed east toward the oil fields. The reporters were thwarted in their attempt to follow the action by roadblocks on the only road leading to the fields. They were left with nothing they could put on the air except long distance shots of plumes of smoke from the burning buildings and ships and the incredible eyewitness accounts. Most of the eyewitness accounts were not broadcast because they were too unbelievable. No animal could cause all this they reasoned. Also since they were broadcasting live they couldn't afford to put more foolish stories on the air which they would later have to retract.

Stunned at the amount of damage he saw General Jasiri ordered an immediate combined Army and Air Force response. His first objective in the Majini area was to block the reported animal attack from reaching the oil fields. His next objective was the destruction of the animal.

The General was a man who believed brute force could stop any enemy or solve any problem. If that didn't work then it meant you didn't apply enough force, so use more. A lifetime of studying and witnessing what war can do had hardened him. He saw the suffering and death it caused, especially wars that dragged on for years. He developed a philosophy that said use overwhelming force at the beginning of a conflict to end it as soon as possible.

At the oil fields the creature was ready to make his move. Lightning was a known cause of oil fires but he didn't know this. He also didn't know it but the enterprising Ashantians had connected their wells together in an interlocking pattern. They had linked their wells together eight at a time to more efficiently move the oil. So every well was connected to seven additional wells. Not knowing this the creature reached out one of his front feet and changed part of the matter in it to sheer energy. He held it close to a well head and a charge of electricity bolted out that was equal in force to a bolt of lightning. He was delighted when he was rewarded with a huge explosion from the well. It was followed by a rapid chain reaction which ignited the seven attached wells. Large oil fires erupted from the wells producing towering flame and ugly dirty black clouds. As he rapidly went from one cluster of wells to another he repeated the procedure. The scene quickly became eerily reminiscent of the Kuwaiti oil fires of the first Gulf War back in the last century.

As all the burning and confusion was building the Army mechanized and tank divisions arrived on the scene. They had been briefed on what to expect but were taken aback by the sight of what was taken place in front of them. However, they quickly organized into attack formations. Their orders were to wait for the Air Force to finish their attack then follow up if needed. A few minutes after they were in position two waves of F-35's flew overhead. These were all the planes they were able to get off the ground but were considered more than enough. One formation of five jets peeled off to attack while the other five jets circled overhead. This time they were prepared and loaded for bear. They knew what the target was this time and picked their ordinance carefully. As a result they were not limited to what could fit in their internal bays, but used the full range of weapons available. Under their wings hung laser guided bombs, air to ground missiles and heavier cluster bombs than used in the previous attack. There was no real need to dive on the target. With their smart munitions they could just lock on the target and release or fire the ordinance while maintaining their altitude.

The creature saw the planes, tanks and troops. He wasn't concerned; he had proven his point that their weapons couldn't hurt him. This time he didn't feel like being interfered with by their ordinance exploding against his body. As the jets began their turn toward him he changed his outer skin from matter to energy and formed a type of energy shield around him. The air around him seemed to take on a thin, green, yellowish glow. This glow was very faint and not apparent to any but the keenest observers. However, a few witnesses were able to see this and report it later.

Elisha Washington and her hastily put together news crew of herself, one cameraman and the pilot, arrived over Majini at this time and began filming the carnage, smoke and flames. They could see jets flying and circling in the distance.

"Leesh," said Rob her helicopter pilot. "I'm picking up warnings on the radio. The military is ordering all civilian air traffic away from the Majini area. We need to turn back."

"Don't turn back now, this looks like the biggest story of the year."

"But we've been ordered to turn back. We could lose our license to fly in this country."

"Just don't answer them. Act like you didn't

hear the message. We have to get this story."

"Ok if you say so, the boss said go along with what the reporter asks on a story. But I'll tell you what; if it looks too dangerous to me I'm turning around and getting the heck out of there, story or no story."

Leesh turned to her cameraman, Jake.

"Is the studio getting our live transmission yet?"

"Yeah, they're getting it but we're not on the air yet."

"What's the hold up?"

Leesh was excited but also worried that they would be chased away from the story of a lifetime. She made contact with Mark Hammond in the studio herself.

"Mark, we have to go live now. I don't know how much longer we can stay here."

"We're trying to get on now Leesh," he replied. "Give me five more minutes."

The young reporter was getting nervous. Things were not happening the way she planned. Events were happening too fast and she had the unnerving feeling maybe she had bit off more than she could chew. But no, this was her big chance and she is not going to blow it. They are getting her feed she reasoned and standard procedure is to record all live, on location broadcasts. These are stored in the SNN library just in case they are needed later. So anything they are shooting now can still be broadcast, just not live. Leesh turned to Rob.

"Rob we have got to get shots of whatever is happening in the distance where those jets are circling."

She noticed more and thicker, black smoke was rising from that general area. There was a lot more smoke now in that direction than when they first arrived. Events were moving fast, maybe too fast.

"Let's get a swing over the harbor and wharf area then head for the area where all the military activity is happening," said Leesh.

As the crew flew over the carnage in the port the word came from the studio they were now live. Leesh began her voiceover and narration of what was unfolding below them.   She began to wonder what her parents back in VA Beach will think when they see this report. Will they worry? After all she had calmed their worries over her moving here by convincing them she was going to one of the safest places in the world. After all nothing ever happens in Ashanti. I guess we'll never be able to say that again, she thought. She forced all these thoughts behind her and tried to deliver her voice in a professional manner. But should she dare mention the eyewitness reports they picked up from the local stations? Witnesses had reported a huge animal had caused all of this. If the accounts were proven wrong and she broadcast them, a mistake like that could really hurt her career. On the other hand, what if it turns out to be true and she didn't report it? She decided she had a duty to report the claims no matter how wild they sounded. At the end of her report on the destruction in the port area Leesh paused, then signed inwardly. Well here goes nothing.

"There has been no word from the government on what caused the chain of explosions and fires. In fact the news media have been unable to get the government to respond to any questions about the cause of the catastrophe. Government spokesmen will only say it is believed hundreds are dead and relief efforts are underway. Indications seem to show there was some sort of explosion in the oil transfer facilities on the wharfs that caused a chain of explosions and fires in the port. But that doesn't explain how widely separated ships in the harbor are also in flames and sinking. I would be remiss if I didn't report to you that local eyewitness accounts say a large creature or monster caused all of this damage. I know it sounds crazy viewers but numerous individuals keep reporting the same seemingly ridiculous story. We're going to move now to an area in which it looks like there is heavy military activity and try to get footage of what's going on there. This is Elisha Washington reporting for SNN News."

The network went to a long commercial break until she and her news crew was in their new position. As soon as she got the signal she was off the air Leesh turned to Rob.

"Ok, let's get over there to the area where the jets are circling."

Her stomach felt like it was full of butterflies. Now that she was off the air she began to think about what she was doing.

Am I crazy? This is more than I expected. This whole area looks like a nightmarish hell. And here I am flying into who knows what. This is dangerous; I could get killed doing this. Maybe I should count my blessings and head back to the studio. But the story is still out there and whatever is out there is not being reported. This is my job and I have to do this.

CHAPTER 13

Back at the military command center General Jasiri was watching the SNN broadcast. They had switched to commercials and previously recorded footage of the events. Apparently they were killing time until they moved to a different position. He questioned one of his nearby aids.

"What's the progress of our attack?"

"It's just started. No reports are in yet. But we may have a problem with the SNN helicopter. It's ignoring our calls to leave the exclusion zone and is now heading for the battlefield area."

"Are you sure they hear our warnings4?"

"They're acting like they don't hear us but we're transmitting on all the frequencies they should be monitoring. We're pretty sure they hear us but are acting like they don't."

"Well, keep warning them off but take no other action toward them. As long as they don't get in the way leave them alone. If they want to kill themselves let them. Anyway, we're getting better pictures from them than we are from anywhere else."

Leaving nothing to chance the first wave of jets fired their missiles and dropped their bombs on the creature. They were fully expecting nothing to be left of him but pieces of raw meat and blood. Their ordinance appeared to be on target. There was no real problem with target acquisition, despite all the increasing smoke from the oil fires. The animal disappeared from view because of all the explosions; it was a piece of cake. But as the smoke cleared from all the detonations the unbelievable became apparent. He was still standing and walking with no obvious injuries. Even worse he continued to set more oil wells ablaze while they watched. He wasn't even slowed down. The second wave was quickly called down to attack.

In the middle of their attack Leesh and the SNN crew arrived on the scene. She was immediately put on live and her narration was broadcast to all the affiliates worldwide. In Europe and Africa where it was morning people were watching the curious and mysterious events. However, in the U.S. and North and South America the majority of people were still in bed sleeping. They were woefully ignorant to the unfolding and shocking events that could soon threaten the whole world. Leesh couldn't see what the military was attacking from her location because of all the smoke and the distance. Nevertheless she reported what she saw from her unique aerial vantage point.

There were more explosions as more ordinance was released on the creature from the jets, again with no results. The scene had become nightmarish as much of the ordinance had set off more oil fires instead of stopping the creature. That, plus the fires the creature started left the area in a Dante like inferno. Fires and thick black smoke were everywhere. The smoke was becoming so thick it was beginning to block out the sun. Unburned oil began to drop from the sky like black rain.

On the ground the troops and tanks moved in to do what was supposed to only be a mopping up operation if the creature was merely wounded. They were close enough to see the creature and everything that happened in the previous attacks. They had both fear and anger in them at the idea of being sent on what looked more and more like a suicide mission. They saw what happened when the jets attacked. What good would their small arms do against this monster? But with the tanks leading the way they pressed ahead.

Back at the SNN control center Sam had come in from his day off to coordinate the handling of the story. He was a little worried because he knew the story would be seen live by millions of people. If mistakes were made on the air Leesh would probably be unfairly blamed for them. He didn't want the label amateurish put on her. That was something that could haunt her for years. He decided to stop the live broadcast, edit the remainder of the report and show an edited version on the air.

"Rob," said Leesh, "we can't see what they're attacking from here. It's too much smoke and we're too far away. We have to get closer."

"You may be in a hurry to get killed but I'm not," replied Rob. "They're using heavy ordinance in there, and look at all that smoke. The smoke is beginning to block out the sun. What if some idiot thinks we are the enemy and takes a couple of pot shots at us? It wouldn't take much to bring down this chopper. Even if they don't bring us down the metal on this thing is as thin as paper. Even a .22 bullet would probably go straight through us."

"Rob, how about one quick dash to get us in range? Just give us one or two minutes to get a shot of the object of all this fighting. No other network has that yet and we would be the first. We would scoop everyone."

Rob thought for a long few seconds then answered.

"Ok, maybe I'm crazy too but I'll do it. But I'm only going to stay close for one minute. Jake, you better get your money shot fast because I'm not going to hang in there any longer than that."

Rob tried to pick an area that had the least amount of smoke and flew a course that would get him close to the battlefield and insure them a clear view. He was not helped by the shifting winds which moved around the massive black clouds of smoke. At times he was in the clear but at other times the visibility was near zero. The closer he got, the more he could feel the concussions from the tank and artillery rounds.

Leesh gave a running narration of what she saw to her viewers while Jake recorded the video. She described the dramatic scene which included all the oil fires which seemed to be increasing by the minute. Sometimes the smoke would clear and the crew would get a good view of the tanks firing and slowly advancing. But so far all they could see of the intended target were the explosions because of the all-encompassing and shifting smoke. The chopper was so close now it shook with every new explosion.

"Rob," said Leesh over the intercom, "we have to get closer. We aren't getting any good pictures of what there're attacking from here."

"Have you lost your mind? The fillings in my teeth are starting to shake loose now. I've just about had all I can take in here."

"Come on Rob, we didn't come through all this to leave without the main shot we want. We have to get at least one shot of the enemy."

"Well hold on to your hats. I'm going to make a high speed pass directly over the target. Jake, you better make it good. I'm making one pass then we're heading home. We've pushed our luck enough and we're running low on fuel anyway."

Rob started his run and advanced his controls to get the most speed he could out of the helicopter. More shock waves rocked the aircraft as they neared the area where all the explosions were centered. The heavy black smoke was everywhere. It began to look like the only good view must be from the ground. Rob was beginning to second guess his actions. Why did he let a reporter who was still wet behind the ears get him into this situation? As they passed directly over the target the smoke briefly cleared. Something was down there and it was big, very big.

"What in the world? I saw something," said Leesh. "It looked like a huge head and a torso of an animal. I only saw it for a second but it almost looked like a dinosaur. But that couldn't be right. Did anyone else see it?"

"Naw," said Rob. "I didn't see anything except smoke. I was too busy flying the aircraft."

"Jake," said Leesh, "did you get a shot of it?"

"I'm not sure. I saw something flash by through my viewfinder, but I don't know what it was."

"Well whatever it was we're getting out of here and heading back to the studio," said Rob.

Rob turned the aircraft in a heading for the studio on a course that gave a wide berth to the battle area. He wanted nothing more to do with this and had experienced enough excitement for today. Leesh opened her mouth and started to try to talk him into one more look, but thought the better of it and let it go. He was right. It would have been foolish to push the envelope any further. It was time to call it a day and go home.

The military on the ground however, didn't

109

have the luxury of calling it a day. The tanks followed by the ground troops continued to close on the creature. The creature was getting tired and bored with the whole affair. All the wells he could see were in flames. He had destroyed or severely damaged the country's capacity for producing and moving oil through its main port. Unless they got massive help it will take years to put out the fires and repair the damage. Also, they are not going to get much help from their main benefactor the U.S. or the rest of the world. He has plans for the rest of the world that will keep them more than occupied with their own self interests. He was sick of the stench of burning oil and he had dirty black oil all over him. It was time to end this and get back to the sea, but he had a couple of loose ends to take care of first.

The line of troops and tanks were still advancing on him. Their fire plus the artillery fire from unseen positions in the rear were still raining down. Their fire was having no effect but it irritated him that they wouldn't give up and kept closing on him. He could see the humans still weren't really afraid enough of him yet. Ok, now it was time to humble, humiliate and shock the humans.

The creature turned toward the advancing forces quickly closing the distance. He ripped into the line of tanks. In a frenzy of activity he crushed, overturned and tossed heavy main battle tanks as if they were toys. Some he picked up and slammed into each other as if he was using one walnut to crack open another. He was hit at point blank range with armor piercing shells but none of them could get past his all-powerful shield.

Then in the final insult to humble the humans he went after the troops following the tanks. The troops showed great bravery and held their ground while continuing to fire with their rifles and machine guns. However, when he reached the soldiers he grabbed whole handfuls and began to eat them. The helmets they wore were like hard seeds in a grape to him so as he ate the troops he let the helmets drop out of his mouth, some of them with the heads still attached. At this devastating sight and with the knowledge their weapons had shown no effect even the most hardened soldier's heart grew faint. As he continued to plow into their ranks and feed on the troops they broke and ran in pure panic from the gory sight. All military discipline collapsed and the troops fled, many dropping their weapons and running for their lives.

Daylight broke over Washington. It was a dark and dreary day in the nation's capital. The sky was full of dark clouds and it was raining cats and dogs. It was in sharp contrast to the previous days of sunny beautiful weather that the capital had been enjoying lately.

The phone rang in the bedroom of President John Logan waking him and his wife Susan. He awoke irritated and looked at his clock. It was 7:10 am. Who was calling him this early on a Saturday morning? This was his day for sleeping late and his staff knew it. He groggily reached for and picked up the phone. On the line was the voice of George Bradley, his White House Chief of Staff.

"Mr. President, I 'm sorry to wake you but I think you need to turn on your TV and tune it to SNN."

"Why, what's going on George?"

"Well it's kind of hard to explain that's why I didn't call you earlier. It seems to be some sort of catastrophe in Ashanti. Their major oil fields have been set ablaze and their oil transfer facilities have been just about destroyed."

"What?" He quickly reached for his remote. "Who did this? You people told me the country was stable, that's why I sold them all that fancy military hardware."

"Mr. President this is the hard part, SNN is reporting it may have been some sort of animal that caused all of this."

"What are you talking about George? What kind of a news organization are they running there? What does their government and the local media say?"

"The government is tight lipped and is only saying the events are under investigation and rescue operations are under way. The local media is saying it was a gigantic monster."

"What kind of foolishness is this? For heaven's sake, we get most of our oil from there. Call our ambassador there and tell him to get to the bottom of this. Then call the Chairman of the Joint Chiefs and tell him to call all his military contacts in Ashanti and find out what he can learn. And get the CIA and NSA in on this thing. Why didn't they see this coming and what do they know? Then I want you to call a meeting with both the Chairman of the Joint Chiefs and the Cabinet. I want it scheduled for today, ASAP."

The President was angry and alarmed. What could have caused this? He watched the scenes of smoke, fire and destruction being shown on TV. It looked like a war zone over there. This was no accident, it had to be deliberate, and it had to be some sort of attack or sabotage. Was Ashanti attacked by another country? Whatever the reason is we'll soon find out. If it was outside forces that did this the U.S. may be forced to respond. Ashanti and its oil are vital U.S. interests and I can't allow any country to so boldly interfere with our free flow of oil.

"John, what's happening over there?"

He was slightly startled at his wife's questioning voice. He was so deep in thought he had almost forgotten she was in the room.

"I'm not sure myself. What you see on TV is just about all I know."

As he hurriedly showered and dressed his stomach turned over at the thought of what effect this could have on the American economy.

In Ashanti, General Jasiri was shocked at the reports he was receiving. He was amazed that his forces couldn't stop or even hurt the creature. When he received reports that the monstrous animal was deliberately eating his troops he hung his head. This is a complete disaster for his country. And his poor troops, what effect was this going to have on their morale and confidence? He began to hate the animal or monster or whatever it is. He received word in his latest report the thing is heading for the unoccupied coastal area to the west. Since there is nothing in that area and it is the shortest way to the ocean, it must mean its returning back to the sea.

Good riddance, he was glad it is leaving. This is no ordinary animal. This thing is pure evil and not only that, it has to be intelligent. His military hit it with just about every weapon at its disposal and nothing even hurt him and these were the best weapons, American weapons. This thing ignored the population centers and attacked only areas that were economically the most important to the country. This thing has some kind of agenda or plan. Killing people wasn't his main objective; it only attacked his forces when they pressed their attack too close to him. This happened in the incident with the patrol boat and with the Army's tank and troop attack. He made a quick decision that he knew would be criticized, but he had seen enough useless loss of life for one day.

"Order our forces to reorganize and make a stand on the other side of the river," ordered the General. "Send out a recon force to follow it and make sure it leaves, but do not attack it. I want this message sent out to all forces. Let the thing go and don't take any more offensive action against it. And tell the patrol boats off the coast to let it through, give it a wide berth."

The General had sized up his adversary and had a feeling he knew what it was going to do. He felt it had accomplished its goal and was now only interested in leaving. Unless they provoked it the freak of nature was going to leave without causing any further damage. It will be better to let it go and let him become someone else's problem. His country had suffered enough this day.

The recon unit followed the creature to the coast, filming and recording his action from long distance. He noticed how wary the humans were of him now. They had stopped attacking him and with a new sense of fear seemed afraid to approach him too closely. Good, they're learning. He knew others had to be taught however, especially the most confident and arrogant country on this world. It was the one most of the others looked up to as the most powerful. The European Union almost equaled them in power but this country stood alone and shared its power with no one. Even though many of the countries in the world resented this one they still looked up to them. Once he vanquished them it would put fear and hopelessness in the others. This country prized and valued money more than anything else, even though they denied it. That would be his target, their money. They called this country the United States. Once he humbles this country the rest will see the hopelessness of resisting him.

He reached the edge of the ocean which met high rugged cliffs on the coastline. He gazed down at the water below. He could sense the water was deep here and he could dive into the water below without hitting the bottom. Before he left there was one more surprise he would give the humans. He felt they couldn't stop him even if they knew his next target. So, it amused him to tease them and give them one more shock. He decided to give them a hint of his next target if they can figure it out. He also knew it will scare the daylights out of them when they realized he can talk. He turned to the recon unit following him and with the loudest voice he could summon he spoke these words, "I GO TO THE WALL." With those words he turned, dove into the water and swam away.

Back at the Command Center there was pandemonium when the last report was received from the recon unit. The monstrous animal had actually talked. He spoke in English which he learned from the brain of Dr. Peterson. In fact he gained the memory and knowledge from the brain of every person he devoured. So in effect he was gaining more and more information about this world and its people every time he ate another human. English was a second language in Ashanti and taught in their secondary schools, so he was understood by most of the people who heard the curious words. However, what did I go to the wall mean; in fact did it have any meaning at all?

General Jasiri ordered all recordings made of the creature, especially the last one of him talking, classified top secret. This is no normal animal, that has been verified as a fact now. No animal can talk, make intelligent decisions and do the things this one has done. There is something monumental going on here and this has to be just the opening act. Until they analyze the information they have and get a better understanding of what they are dealing with, they have to put a lid on this. If the general public knew all of this there could be panic and hysteria throughout the world.

CHAPTER 14

At SNN headquarters in Atlanta, the last scene of footage which showed what some interpreted as the head and torso of an animal was ordered not to be shown on the air. It was filmed through heavy smoke and the helicopter was moving at high speed when it was taken. Many people who saw the footage said it didn't look like anything other than another smoke cloud. The technicians were ordered to pull out a better image.

Hours later a contentious and boisterous White House meeting ended without a clear answer to the fantastic, ground swelling events that occurred earlier in the day. President Logan was not happy with the answers he got from anyone. Despite repeated inquires the government and military of Ashanti was not very forthcoming with information on what caused the disaster. They had classified all of their intelligence and recordings top secret and for the time being wouldn't release them to the United States.

The proud people of Ashanti were embarrassed and humiliated. They were not in a mood to share their findings with the outside world yet. They had to examine and reflect on what happened and what they did wrong before they would talk about today's events. The Ashantians knew the culprit in this whole affair was an animal. They were very sensitive at the thought of how the rest of the world was going to react when it was revealed they couldn't stop this creature.

The meeting ended with Logan reminding everyone that the free flow of oil from Ashanti was responsible for the great health of the American economy, and nothing was going to be allowed to interfere with that. He ordered the State Department, military and intelligence agencies to gather any information they could through their sources and report it at the next meeting in twenty four hours.

Later that day when President Logan called the President of Ashanti personally to extend his condolences and pledge of support even he ran into the wall of secrecy. The Ashanti leader was evasive and would only say the events are under investigation. Here was a man the U.S. President thought he had developed a relationship with stonewalling him. Rather than press the issue, due to the enormity of the tragedy he backed off for now. However, he wanted answers and he was not going to wait very long for them.

Meanwhile the creature was on a course swimming for North America. He was back to his routine of eating and gorging on sea life. Whenever he was full he again began to kill for the sake of killing. It was almost fun for him.

President Logan changed his meeting plans for the next day and decided on a smaller follow up meeting. After all with the entire cabinet there they still couldn't give him any good answers. He instead scheduled a meeting with his two most trusted people, Secretary of State Adams and Joint Chiefs Chairman Hartsfield. He also included his White House chief of staff and the NSA and CIA head in the meeting. The previous attendees submitted reports which the chief of staff had the dubious task of shifting through looking for something useful.

Twenty four hours later President Logan started his meeting in the Situation room of the White House.

"Ok," said the President, "tell me what we know now." "What happened yesterday?"

Secretary Adams spoke first. "Well as far as what the Ashanti government is telling us they are saying the same thing as yesterday which is really nothing. They're starting to float some sort of weak cover story about a possible separatist or terrorist attack but I don't give any credence to that. I'm sure they know full well what happened but just aren't talking."

"General Hartsfield, what did you learn?" said the President.

"Top secret has been stamped on everything about this. We're not having any more success with our military contacts than before," said Chairman Hartsfield. "It's the weirdest thing; people who we have worked with for years and have always given us information, top secret or not, are clamming up. They seem defensive and embarrassed about the whole situation. But I can tell you this, they admitting to suffering thousands of troops and civilians dead."

"Oh, if they think they are going to get away with not telling us what they know they better think again," said President Logan. "All that modern military hardware we sold them and all the help they are going to expect from us to rebuild says they are going to tell us everything they know. But first I want to hear what we know from our intelligence people. NSA and CIA you have the floor. What do you know?"

Alexander McCarran, the NSA director spoke first. "We are pretty sure we know what caused this but it's still hard for us to believe it ourselves. So, bear with me and let me tell you what we have first. We just like the rest of you first heard of all this on TV. We saw the SNN broadcast showing all the damage and mayhem over there. We were curious about who was reporting the story. No one had ever seen a reporter called Elisha Washington until yesterday. It turns out she is basically a rookie and only got on the air because no other reporter was at the studio yesterday. By the way yesterday was their Foundation Day celebration so it couldn't have happened on a worst day."

President Logan cut off the NSA chief. "You say you know what happened, well get to the point."

"Yes Mr. President, like I said our first information was the same as everyone else, from the SNN broadcast. Later we started searching our resources. One of our satellites over the South Atlantic which looks for SIGINT, which is signal intelligence, basically recorded the whole thing."

"Well why didn't you say something before now?"

"Sir, the truth is we didn't know we had anything. Our filtering programs labeled it as possible military exercises and tagged them for storage. What we got was military traffic and chatter discussing their combat operations which were in progress."

"What did they say?"

The President was getting more and more impatient with his NSA chief. He was taking too long to get to the point. He was acting like he almost didn't want to say what he found.

"Mr. President we picked up action reports from patrol boats off the coast, jets, troops, tanks and even a C-130 on a training mission. They were all broadcasting out in the open and weren't even coding their transmissions. This is the fantastic part; they all described fighting some kind of huge animal."

"Wait a minute, you mean to tell me an animal caused all of this?"

"Yes sir, I hate to be the one to tell you but that appears to be the case. We only have radio traffic to show this but they seem to be completely genuine."

"Well if it was just an animal why in the world didn't they just kill the thing?"

"The intercepts we have say they hit this thing, which some of them called a monster, multiple times. They claimed hits with every type of weapon in their arsenal including missiles, cluster bombs, 1000 pound bombs and tank anti-armor rounds. You name it; they used it and all to no effect."

"General Hartsfield, are these people incompetent or is it they just don't know how to use the weapons we sold them?"

"Mr. President, we trained them on the weapons before they were released to them and they passed all of the qualifications we required. We gave them the same training we give our troops. They appeared to grasp everything that was taught them and showed good proficiency on everything we sold them. And I must say with the lethality of these weapons you shouldn't have to score a direct hit to kill any animal. All they should have needed to do was just score a near miss. I'm at a loss to explain how this thing could survive an encounter with their military."

"Do we have a picture of this thing?"

Rufus Hobby, the CIA chief answered. "We don't have a picture but we are sure they have one. They should have gun camera footage from their F-

35's and they engaged it at close quarters with their ground units. The information the NSA shared with us indicated they followed it to the coast with a recon unit. I'm positive they have good recordings of it from the oil fields to the coast."

"By the way Mr. President," said the NSA chief. "We think SNN has an image of the animal. We noticed they were broadcasting live initially then latter went to a delayed telecast. That would enable them to edit their broadcast without anyone noticing. We think they never showed the end of their recording when they were near the battle area. We think they're holding it for some reason and don't want to show it."

"Oh, they don't want to show it, huh." The President turned to his chief of staff. "George, get someone to call SNN headquarters. Tell them to give us a copy of any footage they took of this affair. No, tell them to give us the originals, let them keep the copies. Our people may need the originals to enhance them. Tell them it's a national security issue and we appreciate their cooperation. If they hesitate let them know we are not taking no for an answer. Does anybody have anything else?"

A quick look around the room showed no response from the attendees.

"Ok, this meeting is adjourned."

The next day executives at SSN headquarters were surprised to have a call from the White House telling them agents were on the way over to pick up any footage they took in Ashanti of the disaster. They especially asked for the complete footage including any unaired or edited portions. After quick calls to the network owner and CEO William Fentress, he decided against a freedom of the press fight and ordered his people to give the government whatever they wanted. Fentress's people had tried but couldn't

122

get a good image from the recording, which had been flown to the U.S. overnight. Maybe the government with its unlimited resources could do a better job. Also, there was no profit in fighting this on ideological grounds. The bottom line for his stockholders was profit, and there was none in fighting the government.

CHAPTER 15

President Logan awoke from an uneasy sleep. It had been a week since the attack in Ashanti and they still didn't have any clear answers. The story had disappeared from the daily headlines and the news turned somewhere else. To the public there were more interesting events in the news now, like the latest murder or the latest celebrity gossip. He had travel scheduled for political events to prop up election bids by at risk members of his party and he wanted hard information on this affair before he left Washington. The oil fires were still raging in Ashanti but, the images were no longer shown on TV. The public still didn't know it was an animal that caused all of this but the government knew. The President felt he needed more information before the public could be let in on the secret. For goodness sakes, thought the President, we don't even know what the thing looks like.

The smoke obscured images on the SNN footage were a disappointment. The most they were able to get from it was the faint outline of what appeared to be a head and what looked like part of the torso of animal. There seemed to be some faint glow around the animal which was attributed to the effect of sunlight and reflections coming through the heavy and all-consuming smoke clouds. It added more distortion to the generally poor quality of the image. What they could get from the picture was the fact that this was no ordinary animal and it was huge. The public was going to have to be told soon, so now it's time to take the gloves off with Ashanti. They have to possess usable pictures of this thing. President Logan sent instructions to his ambassador in Ashanti to get an audience with their President. He was to put in polite but firm terms that the future cooperation and help from the U.S. depends on the mutual trust and sharing of information on this incident. He was to let them know in no uncertain terms the U.S. wants to see everything they have on this creature ASAP.

Logan was interrupted in his thoughts by a call from Secretary of State Adams. When others weren't around he and Adams talked to each other on a first name basis because of their long relationship.

"John, the Ashanti government wouldn't give our ambassador there a timely meeting with their President, so I called him myself and talked to him directly. I let him know I was speaking for you as per our last conversation. He understands now that the amount of cooperation he gets from us for rebuilding depends on the timely and complete sharing of all the information they have on this creature. I'm happy to say he agreed to send us all their combat footage and any other footage or recordings they have on this animal."

"Excellent, when can we expect to see it?"

"Because of the sensitive nature of this they insist on not transmitting it to us. They're still smarting about all this and want us to hand carry it back to the states. They don't want to take the chance other countries will see this yet. It's being brought here on one of our C-117's we have stationed there and will be here in the morning."

"What's wrong with these people? Are they paranoid, eventually everybody is going to find out about this anyway?"

"Yea, I know you're right but they insist we not show it to any other country without their ok, that is unless the animal poses an immediate danger to another country. I went along with it figuring we could talk them out of it later."

"You did the right thing Clarence; the most important thing for now is to find out what happened."

"By the way John, their President said the strangest thing to me at the end of our conversation."

"What was that Clarence?"

"He said he was sending us copies of everything they have on the monster, as he called it. Then he said, you asked for this so I'm giving it to you, but you may wish you never saw this."

"What did he mean by that?"

"I have no idea, and then he hung up."

The leaders of Ashanti were too busy trying to put out all the oil fires and recover from the terrible devastation they suffered, to care about the creature or where it went. Their biggest headache was the slowness of the world's response to their request for aid, especially their request for the specially trained oil well fighters. They were particularly irritated with the slowness of the Americans to their requests. As a result they were beginning to rethink the wisdom of their close relationship with the United States.

The next morning the footage from Ashanti was delivered in the U.S. for study and analysis. Later that night an emergency meeting was held in the White House Situation Room to show the results of the analysis to the President, military leaders and key participants. The attendees were seated and waiting when the President and his chief of staff entered.

"Don't get up," said President Logan as he took his seat. Once seated he turned to the military intelligence people who were giving the briefing.

"Ok, let's get started."

A tall and rather thin Air Force type who introduced himself as Major Bragg began the briefing. He started with a lot of detailed information on the handling and processing of the footage but, noticing the bored expressions of the participants, especially the President; he quickly skipped over to the actual presentation.

"I have to say in all my years of intelligence I have never seen anything like you are about to see. Brace yourself for what you are about to witness. This briefing is going to concentrate on the military actions against the animal. They sent us large amounts of material that had to do with the damage it caused and casualties but we are not showing you those today. We organized what you are going to see into the actual sequence in which they took place."

The lights dimmed slightly and Major Bragg began showing combat footage on the large monitors in the room. It started with gun camera footage from the first F-35 attack in Majini. There was a simultaneous gasp throughout the room as the creature was clearly seen moving on the ground. It seemed to stop, look up and wait for the ordinance dropped from the jets to hit him. The explosions around it were clearly seen on the screen. The last shots showed it walking away as if nothing had happened.

"Stop," said President Logan, "wait a minute." The lights raised and the presentation stopped.

"What is this, some kind of joke? This can't be

real."

"I felt the same way when I first saw it myself," said the Major. "But we did exhaustive tests on the images and we couldn't find any evidence of doctoring or manipulation. The quality of the images was also consistent with the type of media and recording equipment they use. For example, the gun camera footage was the type of media and consistent with the results you would get from the recording equipment used on the F-35. The images from the recon units were also compatible with what we would expect from the media and recording equipment their recon units use. We are very confident the images are real."

"This is unbelievable," said the President, "By all means continue."

The lights were dimmed again and the presentation continued. The scenes continued showing the conflict of last week. The room was hushed as the mayhem and destruction was played out in flickering color images. The atmosphere was somber as the death and carnage played out on the large screens in the room. When he reached the last scene, just before the creature dove into the water, the Major halted the presentation briefly.

"Gentlemen," he said. Pay particular attention to the last few seconds of this recording." He resumed the playback and to the amazement of the participants the animal spoke these words, "I GO TO THE WALL."

A cascade of noise engulfed the room. Several people jumped up from their chairs. There were loud incoherent discussions all around the room. President Logan brought the briefing back to order.

"Ok, everybody calm down. Major Bragg, that last portion, please tell me it was some kind of voice over that was added to the recording."

"I'm afraid not sir, we feel it is authentic and part of the original recording."

"Are you trying to tell me this thing can talk?"

The major appeared very uncomfortable with the question but knew he had to give an answer. All eyes in the room were fixed on him.

"All our examinations of this footage show no evidence of doctoring. It appears to be real."

Again there was noise and rumblings throughout the room as individual conversations broke out around the table.

"Questions," said the President. "General Hartsfield, what is your analysis of what you saw on the films?"

"I must say Mr. President; I am amazed at what I saw today. This is like nothing I have ever seen. I was leaning toward being critical of the performance of the Ashanti military when we didn't have all the facts, but I must say this puts a different light on things. I don't know what kind of animal this could be but I saw at least several direct hits with heavy ordinance on this thing. There is no way any living thing could survive that. I understand there was no video of it but one of their patrol boats hit it with an anti ship missile at the start of all this and it reacted by sinking the vessel. Just a near miss by one of these weapons should have done the job."

"Then how do you explain it wasn't even scratched?"

"I can't explain that Mr. President, but I do have another observation. The damage it caused, the slaughter of their troops and their inability to even hurt the thing must have had a terrible effect on their military's confidence. You can tell the photographs of him leaving were taken at extreme range. And even though they still had many more additional forces they could have used, they didn't even attempt to continue the engagement when it decided to leave. It looks like they just gave up and let the animal go. I think either they were completely demoralized by this thing or just calculated it was better to let it go than continue to fight the thing. It looks like they just gave up."

"Well," said President Logan, "that's the difference between us and them. If this thing shows his face over here we'll blow it off the face of the earth, right General."

"Yes sir."

He sounded confident, but deep down inside the General was not so sure of that statement. A few days ago he would have agreed with the President. However, after viewing the videos and reading the combat reports he was worried. Nothing could take that kind of punishment and survive. There is something going on here that they don't understand, and no soldier likes to go into battle not knowing everything he can about his enemy.

"What kind of animal is this?" said President Logan. "I've never seen anything like this."

"Neither have I nor has anyone else," said Linwood Midway, his Presidential Science Adviser. "The truth is from what I have seen there is no animal like that."

"Well how do you explain what we just saw on these screens?"

"I can't, what we just saw as a scientist I would have to say it is impossible."

"And what about this thing talking, how can an animal talk?"

"Well it's not that unusual that an animal can make sounds that seem to be speech to humans.

There are numerous examples in the animal kingdom of animals mimicking human speech. A few well known examples are parrots and cockatoo's. Why even mammals such as dogs have been known to make sounds that appear to be words."

"Are you saying we just saw a hundred foot long parrot?"

"No sir, I'm just saying animals have been known to mimic speech."

"Well, that sounds like a little more than mimicking. His voice sounds like a professor speaking perfect English. And what does he mean when he says; I'm going to the wall?"

"I have people who are looking at that right now," said the CIA chief Rufus Hobby. "I have a special team assigned to look into every aspect of this matter."

"Have they come to any conclusions yet?"

"No sir, they only got their copies of the Ashanti footage two hours ago. But, they are working hard examining all the data."

"By the way," said President Logan, "does anybody have an idea where this thing is headed?"

"The last time it was seen was when it dove into the sea," said General Hartsfield. "According to the Ashanti military it submerged and seemed to be headed west. Their navy briefly picked it up on sonar, but of course it could have easily changed direction either north or south. The truth is we have no idea where it is or where it's headed."

"So it can be detected in the ocean," said Logan. "Then we should be able to find it."

"Well yes and no to that statement Mr. President," said Hartsfield. "Yes we can detect it on sonar but the return is similar to a whale or large marine animal. And there are lots of whales in the ocean since whaling was banned for good near the first part of the century. Another problem is it's a big ocean out there. Unless we know where to look it would be sheer luck to find one animal in the whole ocean no matter how big the animal. Look how big our ballistic missile submarines are and they cruise undetected all the time."

"I'm getting tired of hearing what we don't know and can't do. I want everyone to use whatever resources you have to find out anything you can about this thing and where it is headed."

"Mr. President," said NSA director McCarran, "we do have information that may be relevant to the location issue."

"We understand there is some sort of report or data in NOSA about a strange phenomenon that has been occurring in the ocean for several weeks now. It seems to have to do with large fish kills spanning thousands of miles across the South Atlantic. One of their people there thinks it is being caused by some sort of large marine animal but he seems to have little or no proof of this. His conclusions don't seem to be shared by his superiors and the report hasn't been passed out of the agency. The odd thing about this when I think about it now is the direction he claims these large kills were headed. He said they started off the east coast of South America and were headed for the west coast of Africa. Our team has asked NOSA for all the information they have on this subject. We're also asking for any information they have concerning the South Atlantic that might look unusual for the last two years, no matter how insignificant it may seem."

White House chief of staff George Bradley looked at his watch and nodded toward the President. It was time for the President to leave and go to another of his appointments.

"Gentlemen," he said, "we have a definite situation here." "I've seen enough to know this thing poses a threat to our national security. I want this kept out of the media. I want no leaks or disclosures, all of this is on a need to know basis. I'll make the decision when to go public on this. In the meantime I want weekly reports and any important updates sent to my chief of staff on what you are finding out. I want some fast answers. We need to know what this thing is up to before it may decide to strike again. Gentlemen, this meeting is adjourned."

CHAPTER 16

NOSA section chief Jim Eppley was in his kitchen trying his best to cook something for dinner after a long day at work. While doing so he began to replay today in his mind.

This morning he was in his office looking at the usual reports when his department head called and told him to come to his office. He began to wonder what this was about; he hardly ever calls him to his office. Eppley knocked on the door and was told to enter. Inside were the department chief and two rather stiff, dowdily dressed men in dark suits. They were introduced as security agents for Homeland Security and flashed their badges at him. For the life of him he couldn't remember their names. However, he thought to himself, "they're probably CIA or NSA types, and are just saying they're Homeland Security." They wanted to know everything he knew about the strange animal encounter he had last month and the associated fish kills that accompanied it. They seemed especially interested in the method he used to track its travel and set up a rendezvous point for his probe. He gave them copies of everything he had on the matter and they left.

A half hour later his boss called and told him he was relieved of all his normal duties and was to do nothing but concentrate on trying to track the movements of the animal. He said pressure was coming from the highest level of government to find out where this thing was headed. Eppley knew those types of words usually meant the request was coming from the White House. He was both excited and apprehensive at the idea that someone was interested in his ideas. After all part of his earlier success was just plain luck. Yeah, luck and having a probe in just the right spot to barely intercept the animal. Who knows if he can do it again? And if he can't do it again all of the pressure and blame could be dropped on him. He began to second guess his decision to go on record and formally submit a report on the matter. Maybe he should have kept his big mouth shut for once.

Israeli Prime Minister Daniel Ben-Gurion prided himself on keeping up with worldwide current events. He had a keen mind and was familiar with what was going on all over the world. In the position his country was in he felt he couldn't afford to be caught uninformed.

As a young man his father had fought in the Yon Kippur War. It was a war in which Israel was completely caught off guard and didn't see coming. It was a war which his father often told him Israel came close to losing because of poor intelligence, and Israel can't afford to lose wars. Other countries lose wars and continue to exist, but if Israel ever loses it is the end of Israel.

The public had often made comparisons between the similarity of his name and that of the first Prime Minister of Israel, David Ben-Gurion. It made no difference to them that he had often explained that they were not from the same family and the first Prime Minister's given name was actually Gruen, and then later changed to Ben-Gurion. His family's name actually was Ben-Gurion. Despite that fact, the enemies of Israel were often fond of saying a Ben-Gurion was the first Prime Minister of Israel and a Ben-Gurion was going to be the last Prime Minister of Israel. He was determined that was not going to happen on his watch.

He had raised the level of his intelligence gathering services to a higher level than they had attained at any time in the country's history. He wasn't shy about collecting information by any means, legal or illegal. There was danger wherever he looked.

The one bright hope was the seven year peace treaty they had signed with the Arab states and cosigned by America and a consortium of other countries. He was not in favor of it at first, even after all the arm wringing by the Americans. He was however, slightly shocked at the amount of pressure the Americans put on him to sign. They even went as far as threatening to withdraw all support if he didn't sign. Even then he didn't give in until the Americans guaranteed they would come to their aid if Israel was under serious attack. However, the real underlying factor that pushed him to sign was the Israeli public. They were sick of war and overwhelmingly in support of the treaty. Who was he to stand in the way of their dream of a peaceful future?

Still when he thought about it too much he had an uneasy feeling in his stomach. The U.S. had always been their staunch ally, often standing up for them when the rest of the world was against them. Gradually however, over the last few years he noticed their taste for fighting seemed to be waning, especially after what they used to call the War on Terror was over. They had reduced their armed forces and defense spending tremendously. They had pulled most of their overseas troops back to the states and seemed to be concentrating their resources more on domestic programs than defense issues. It reminded him of the American habit of putting their head in the sand after a long and costly conflict, a luxury Israel could never afford. They did the same thing after WWI, WWII, Korea and the Vietnam War. But, that was in the last century. Surely they have learned the folly of that practice? However, if they don't stand by us with a still hostile enemy and world right at our doorstep and we are attacked------? He shook his head, sometimes I think too much.

His thoughts turned to the curious issue of the strange business in the African country of Ashanti. He had watched with curiosity the events on the SNN network. Something highly unusual had happened there and most of the world had shrugged it off. They thought of it as nothing but the case of an incompetent military which had destroyed their own facilities trying to put down some sort of insurrection or uprising. They conveniently dismissed the whole episode as a case of gross overuse of high tech weapons which unwisely had been supplied to them by the Americans. In less than a week the story disappeared from the headlines. The rumor about a huge animal or monster causing the tragedy was considered laughable and dismissed as hysteria by a few backward and superstitious people.

Something, however didn't feel right about either explanation. His curious nature lead him to ask the U.S. President about the incident during their last conversation on the Middle East situation. After all, the Americans have the closest relationship with Ashanti of any world power. Some would even say they have them in their hip pocket. If anyone knows what really happened it has to be the Americans. But, President Logan gave the same old tired story that the Ashanti government gave to everyone. He also sounded evasive and quickly steered the conversation to other matters. Something is going on and the true facts are not being shared with the rest of the world. But who cares, after all none of this could possibly affect Israel's security, or could it? It's just something about this that makes him feel nervous.

Why won't the Americans talk about it? It may be foolish of him he thought, but he has to know more, let the rest of the world ignore this. He has to find out what happened there. Maybe, thought the Prime Minister, it's time to use our "special assets" and find out what really happened in Ashanti.

Over the years Israel had been very good at getting intelligence from sympathetic citizens of foreign countries. Many times they weren't even recruited but voluntarily came to Israeli officials and offered their services. They risked imprisonment and disgrace in their home countries because they believed in the Jewish state and wanted to see it survive. The Israeli government took extraordinary means to protect their identity and used them sparingly. Just before the seven year treaty was signed, it looked like the country was in danger of being attacked and overrun by a horde of countries. During that time a bumper crop of informants secretly came forth, especially in the United States. Several of them were in the upper levels of U.S. intelligence and the Federal government. These were people with access to secret and top secret information. They were referred to as "special assets" and their identities were protected at all cost. The Prime Minister sent out instructions to his intelligence bureaus, tap into the special assets and find out what really happened in Ashanti.

Several months had passed since Jim Eppley had been given the task of tracking the creature. He was not having much success. It was beginning to look like he had just lucked up on his discoveries the last time. The ocean was huge and his resources limited. He had no more than twelve probes available to him in both the North and South Atlantic. He had no clear place to look and they were spread out all over both oceans. He was not getting any reports from civilian ships at sea like he did the last time either. Why wasn't he getting any reports on fish kills? Did this thing change its habits and stop killing sea life? Or was it simply not traveling in the normal shipping lanes where it would be noticed?

The Joint Chief's chairman, General Mark Hartsfield, was ending a meeting with the chiefs of the Army, Navy, Marines and the Air Force.

"Gentlemen, we held this meeting because the President asked us to go over the plans we have that can be used to defend the country in case this animal decides to attack us. I think we all agree we don't have a plan for a scenario such as this because this is a contingency that was never considered. All of our plans were developed to counter a military or terrorist attack, revolt or uprising. Our civilian leadership thinks we won't have a problem destroying it but I don't feel as confident. I must say I was taken aback at the amount of lethal force that was used in Ashanti on this animal with apparently no effect. That pretty much tells us in the event this thing is fought on U.S. soil we are not going to be able to use small arms effectively. Heavy weapons are going to have to be used which of course poise a risk in populated areas. Does anyone have any thoughts?"

"Yes," said General Cannon, chief of staff of the Army. "Due to the barbarous actions of this animal, and by that I mean the eating of troops, I feel we should keep the possibility of direct contact with ground forces to a minimum. I agree small arms fire seems to be very ineffective on this animal so I feel it is not worth the risk to our troops to have them in close proximity to this thing.

I must strongly state I fear a huge negative psychological effect on our troops if they witness their fellow comrades eaten in from of them. I can't think of any parallel to this in the history of warfare. Who knows what that would do to their morale? I recommend we only use air assets, artillery and tanks, things that can hit at a distance and quickly move out of the way if it approaches. If for some reason we need ground troops in the vicinity they should be in fast armored vehicles, but I would rather not use them anywhere near this thing."

"Any other thoughts?" said General Hartsfield.

"Well I pray if this thing comes ashore it's in a non-populated area," said Air Force chief General Hampton. "Once my boys drop their ordinance, there is no way they can take it back. It's going to hit something and explode. And if people or property are nearby it makes no distinction between friend and foe, it just blows them up. I think most of us have seen the horrible effects overseas when ordinance missed the target. We have all seen civilian casualties and collateral damage caused by errant weapons strikes. We have accepted that as the price of war and imposing our national interests. But think about this, we have not fought on U.S. soil since the Civil War and we have never dropped bombs on American soil.

What are we going to do if this thing comes ashore in a populated area like Washington? Are we going to drop bombs in the middle of Washington? Let's face the fact that no targeting system is 100 percent accurate. Some of our bombs and missiles are going to miss and hit unintended targets like houses, schools, bridges and buildings, just like they do overseas. We all know the American public is not ready for that, so what are going to be our rules of engagement?"

"As for your question about rules of engagement, as of now we don't have any. Our job after this meeting is to have our staffs, after receiving input from us and the White House, come up with a contingency plan to defend the country from this threat. I can say the attitude I got from the White House was drop one bomb and the problem will be solved. I have the feeling there is going to be a lot of resistance to what we finally come up with as a plan. Does anyone else have any other comments or thoughts?"

The Joint Chiefs around the table looked at each other. Several shrugged their shoulders in frustration and in an almost detachment from what was being discussed. They couldn't believe they were sitting at a table discussing plans for the defense of the United States from the threat of an animal. It seemed so ludicrous, they couldn't tell if they should laugh, cry or be insulted. All of the years they had spent in combat and studying their craft didn't prepare them for this. Yet here they were getting ready to prepare themselves to defend the country from attack by an animal. This just has to be impossible, but they all saw the videos and know it to be true. However, knowing something is true and accepting it are two different things. They were still in the early stages of accepting it and felt ridiculous even talking about plans of defense.

"Well gentlemen," said General Hartsfield, "if there are no more comments this meeting is adjourned and our staffs will start contingency planning tomorrow for the defense of the U.S. mainland."

CHAPTER 17

The creature was at midpoint in this leg of his journey. He was approximately half way between the U.S. and Africa. He was still killing and eating fish voraciously to build up and maintain his strength, but had changed his habits somewhat. He had learned a lot from the brain matter of the humans he had digested.

He knew now that the humans didn't eat everything in the sea but only certain types of fish. The other types they considered inedible. He had begun to realize how important sea life was to the wellbeing of these humans and began to look at its destruction as a good way to hurt the humans. So while destroying sea life helped him with his strength it also served a dual purpose of depriving the humans of a prime source of food. Toward this end he also began to realize how interrelated and dependent one form of ocean life was on another for its existence. He didn't have to kill everything, but if he killed the food of one type of animal he could eliminate the entire food chain of several animals.

So he began to kill mainly the fish humans liked and the fish they feed on in their food chain. He also left alone the predators which feed on the humans favorite fish so more pressure would be put on their prime food fish. So to the untrained eye there were less dead fish and mammals in the area where he traveled, but in effect he was getting the same or even a larger negative impact.

Months passed and the world went about its normal business and routines. Babies were born, people were married and people died. There were traffic accidents, plane crashes and all the normal day in and day out activities all over the world. Even the few people who knew of the real danger had begun to relax and subdue their alarm.

Many of them, especially the military, began to think the creature might have been fatally injured or may actually be dead. After all they argued, with all the heavy weapons exploded all around the thing it should have been killed outright. Somehow they reasoned having miraculously survived that, it probably was wounded and is dead somewhere at the bottom of the sea. After all it hasn't been seen or heard from in months. There have been no tale tell signs of it in the oceans and it seems to have disappeared off the face of the earth. Even that geek at the NOSA who claims to have tracked it the last time can't find anything, they argued.

Taking their arguments into account and after weighing the pros and cons of not going public, President Logan decided not to release to the public the information on the creature. Some of his advisors were against his position but he believed there was probably a more than likely chance it was dead.

He was not in the mood to deal with all the questions and hysteria from the press and the public with the midterm elections on the horizon. Getting more congressmen and governors of his party elected right now was his major concern. If this thing is sighted again the government could always explain away its previous non disclosure under the banner of national security and say it was presumed dead. However, he knew there was a slight danger in this approach. The whole thing could blow up in his face if the thing attacked American soil and caused a large amount of death and destruction. So he hedged his bets and ordered the Navy to stand off the eastern seaboard and Gulf of Mexico to give advance warning in case the thing was headed for the U.S. coast.

Jim Eppley was tense and puzzled. He had received scattered reports of dead fish floating on the surface of the sea. The original sightings were near the Bahamas, and then the Gulf Stream, but the latest were off the Mid-Atlantic seaboard. Curiously they were nothing near the magnitude of what was seen the last time. In fact, you could say there was nothing unusual about them. It was not unusual to see dead fish in the quantities that were observed, not unusual at all. There were no probes near the affected areas and he didn't have enough sightings to even attempt a course plot.

Could the animal be headed for the U.S. East Coast? Based on the information he had which was practically nothing, it could be headed for Europe or South America just as easily. If he was pressed for an answer now it would be pure guesswork and he didn't deal in guesswork. In spite of that it's just what his supervisor had been pressing him lately to come up with, a prediction of where the animal was going. As the weeks turned to months more of the big wheels wanted an answer. They wanted to concentrate their meager search recourses in the area where it was most likely to be found.

Although some people inside the government felt it was probably dead they didn't share that with him. In fact, he was told very little about the situation which was still on a need to know basis. He was told simply to track it, nothing else. He just assumed it was the cause of the tragedy in Ashanti, but when he asked he was told he didn't rank high enough to ask questions.

Eppley again looked over the latest reports from the East Coast. They were odd and much different from the reports he received prior to the African incident. The fish kills weren't in the huge numbers as in the past, also everything wasn't killed. Certain species in an area were killed, but other types of species in the same area seemed not to be effected. I need more information to come up with anything. There has to be something they haven't told me that would help. I just can't work like this, he thought. I'm going to have to put my foot down. I'm going to tell them give me everything they have on this thing or they are going to have to find someone else to do this job. I can't do this without more information.

Prime Minister Daniel Ben-Gurion was amazed at the contents of the intelligence report he was reading. One of his "special assets," a member of the U.S. State Department had given him unbelievable intelligence. The rumors were true; the disaster in Ashanti was the work of some huge creature. Not only that, there was also the startling discloser that none of the weapons used against him had any apparent affect.

So his old friends the Americans were holding out on him. They were well aware of the facts and were keeping them to themselves. Not only were they keeping this from Israel but also from the rest of the world and their own people. What a dangerous game the Americans are playing thought, the Prime

146

Minister. They are putting their hopes on the chance that this menace is dead somewhere at the bottom of the sea. Well, let them hope all they want he thought, as for Israel we are not going to sit around and hope this thing doesn't come here. One thing history has shown us is you can't hope a problem away. Unless you do something to solve a problem it's going to come back to haunt you again.

Particularly troubling were allegations that the thing spoke words. An animal that talks, how can there be such a thing? Something epic is happening and sadly there may be worst things to come from this situation he reluctantly concluded.

As always, the State of Israel can't afford to count on anyone else for its security. The Americans have shown they can't be counted on in this matter by the way they kept us in the dark. Israel is going to have to be prepared to defend itself alone and we're going to do just that, but first we need more information. We also need to have a different, possibly unconventional weapon or defense. Doing the same thing others have done will probably get us the same results they got, which was nothing.

Admiral Stevens, Chief of Staff of the U.S. Navy, stood looking at his large wall monitor which showed the worldwide deployment of his ships. He was closely studying his ship deployments off the American east and west coasts and the Gulf of Mexico. On his screen were different colored dots with the different colors representing different types of ships. Under each dot was a letter combination which told him the name of the ship. Its direction, speed, latitude and longitude were also show in different number combinations below the name. Back in the good old days of the 400 ship navy the screen would have been covered with lights. However, with the reality of military downsizing which he had to live with the dots were few and far between.

The President had ordered him to set up an early warning surveillance off the U.S. East Coast and the Gulf. Now how in the world was he supposed to do that with only 200 ships in the whole Navy? With our commitments throughout the world already straining our capability to the limit, where was he going to get the ships? Also he couldn't use just any ships; he was looking for an underwater object. That fact dictated he could only use submarine warfare equipped combat ships. The majority of his navy would be useless for this task.

He had hastily scrambled together a mix of submarines and surface ships. Some had to be rushed out of shipyards and pulled from maneuvers or training. They were quickly sent to positions off the coasts. Most of them were still racing to get to their assigned positions as the big screen indicated. But even when they reached their positions there would be huge gaps between them. There were literally thousands of miles of coast to cover but he could only deploy a little over a dozen ships. More were on the way from overseas deployments, but the most that he could put on this effort now was a total of two dozen ships.

In his estimate it would have to be pure luck to find one lone animal swimming in the ocean without any idea where to look. If he only had an indication where to concentrate his search he would have a chance, but with the way things stood the thing would almost have to come directly at a ship for them to pick it up. No one seemed to listen to him when he clambered for a larger navy for all those years. Although even he had to admit he never anticipated this would be one of the reasons for more ships.

He stopped his scan of his screen and concentrated on the dot representing the nuclear attack submarine USS Florida. Why is the Florida still in port and not in position? He picked up his handset and called one of his aids familiar with the deployment plans.

"Why is the Florida still in port?"

"They're in the middle of a scheduled rearming sir. They're the last sub in the navy to get the new Mark 57 torpedoes and are in the middle of offloading their old Mark 48's and replacing them with the new ones. We thought it would be better to let them finish. We felt if they got into combat it would be best if they had the latest weapons."

"Tell them to cease weapons loading and immediately head to their assigned position. This is primary an early warning mission. It's more important for them to get on station and watch out for this thing."

Aboard the USS Florida Captain James Hancock called his XO Marvin Thomas on his intercom.

"Marv shut down the rearming process and get the boat prepared to go out to sea."

"But sir, we haven't finished loading the new fish yet."

"We don't have time to finish. We've been ordered out immediately. Stop whatever we are doing and prepare to head out to sea. Check the tides and make sure we have enough water under us. We need to leave ASAP. Make the usual preparations and check with the chiefs to make sure we are sea worthy."

"Yes sir, I'm pretty sure most of the crew is on board or on the base."

"Well get a head count and roundup anyone who is missing. We need to be out of here before midnight."

"Aye, aye sir, I'll take care of it. By the way sir, if I may ask what is going on? The men have been hearing about all the ships being sent out of port unexpectedly for the last couple of days. Does this have anything to do with that?"

"I'll tell you what Marv, when you finish getting this ball rolling come to my quarters. I have the craziest story to tell you about our mission and this whole thing."

In his mind Jim Eppley went over the new information he had received over and over again. The government had reluctantly shared with him the only information they had about the creature's direction. The creature had actually talked, this was unbelievable. It not only had talked, but had actually said the phrase, "I go to the wall." No one, not even their greatest code breakers could come up with an explanation of where or what this meant.

He went to his computer, logged into the internet and put the word wall into a search engine. He paused before he pressed the enter key and thought to himself, what am I doing? If the pros can't figure out what this means why am I trying? He shrugged his shoulders and pressed the button anyway. What he got was more information than he would ever need on the word wall. He got a definition of the word wall, businesses with the name wall and all sorts of places with the word wall in it. He got places such as Wall, South Dakota, the Great Wall of China, the Berlin Wall, the Wailing Wall, the Vietnam Veterans Wall and the list went on and on. But he knew he wasn't looking for just any place. He was only looking for places on the U.S. East Coast. After eliminating everything else he came up with the Veterans Wall in D.C., Wall Street in N.Y., Wall N.J. and the Wall of Honor at Ellis Island. All of these places were grouped in the Mid Atlantic or lower New England area just like his last odd reports. Could it be this easy? No, this can't be right, but on the other hand it's all I can come up with as a destination. But why would any of these places be an objective of some monstrous animal? It's not my job to figure out these matters, he thought, my only job is to track this thing and tell them where I think it's going. Ok, they want a destination; I'll give them my best guess.

He picked up his phone and called his boss.

"You said you wanted an answer to where this thing would make landfall. Well I'm calling its destination as the upper Mid Atlantic or Lower New England area, probably between Washington D.C. and N.Y. City."

"When?"

"I don't know; it may already be there. It's an animal; it could show up today or a month from now. Animals are unpredictable, it's not like they think like a human. But if it acts the same way it did the last time, you know doesn't wait around but goes straight in, then I would say it will probably happen in the next seven days."

The word was passed up through the chain of command. A prediction had been made on the creature's next landfall. The geek at NOSA, as he had been called by many, had finally come up with something. The information was met with skepticism at the highest levels of decision making. President Logan and the Joint Chiefs were briefed by their advisors but they saw very little hard evidence to support the prediction made by Eppley. The

President had little confidence in the prediction but felt he couldn't afford to ignore it. He ordered the Navy to beef up its presence in the area between Washington and NYC.

Admiral Stevens was wary of leaving any area of the coast unprotected but he was forced to redeploy ships wherever he could. He decided to collapse the spacing of his ships on the East Coast and have a heavier concentration off the area between DC and NYC. The Admiral decided to leave a token amount of ships in the Gulf of Mexico and move the rest to the East Coast. He would have to sacrifice his coverage off the Southern and northern New England states by removing ships from those areas and squeezing them in at the predicted landfall area. He didn't like it but he gave the orders. In thirty six hours if everything worked smoothly and the weather cooperated his ships would be in their newly assigned positions.

But events have a way of not waiting for the right conditions. In fact most events seem to happen when you're not ready for them.

Captain Hancock was in his Combat Information Center (CIC) on the USS Florida when he received his redeployment orders. He was currently patrolling off the coast near Norfolk, VA. He took a quick look at his current position, then the approximate coordinates of his newly assigned position. He picked up a microphone and patched into his ship wide communications system. He wanted everyone on the ship to know where they were going.

"Men, this is the Captain, I have just received a communication stating all ships in the exercise have been redeployed."

Hancock was careful in his choice of words. Only a few of the crew knew what their real mission was, those with the need to know. He had told most of the crew the authorized cover story that they were participating in a fleet exercise. The object of the supposed exercise was to detect the intrusion into American waters by a nuclear sub of an unnamed rogue nation. The enemy sub was supposedly being simulated by a U.S. submarine. Thus the frantic departure and deployment of the ships up and down the coast was explained away.

Captain Hancock continued, "We have been reassigned to stand off the coast near the entrance to NY harbor."

CHAPTER 18

The sun rose on a bright clear day in New York City. After a week of clouds, rain and overcast the weather was perfect. It was in sharp contrast to the norm for this time of year. There was not a cloud in the sky and the sky was a beautiful shade of blue. Some of the city's older residents said it reminded them of the sky during the September 11th terrorist attacks. It was cloudless and this same beautiful shade of blue during the worst day in the city's history. However they always said that, the events of that time were so etched in their memory that they couldn't stop associating with them, that's at least how older people felt.

Most of the current young residents of the city were either too young to remember those days or hadn't been born when it happened. In addition, they were slightly irritated when their parents kept bringing up the subject whenever the sky looked to them like it did that day. This seemed to happen at least two or three times a year. The annual memorials and wall to wall coverage of the tragedy had finally subsided now to the point where it wasn't taking over everything each September 11th. The city and the nation were beginning to finally leave it behind like an earlier generation had eventually got over the annual Pearl Harbor Day memorials.

Of course none of this meant anything to the huge monstrous thing swimming toward his intended target. He was only concerned with destruction and the accomplishment of his next goal. He was on a mission to destroy as much as he could of what he felt was the American's most prized possession, the symbolic and actual seat of its financial power centered at the Wall Street Financial District.

Up he rose out of the cool dark depths. He raised his head out of the water to look around and get his bearings. He was seeing the city for the first time with his own eyes, but in reality he had seen this all before from the puny man's memory. Somehow it all seemed a little different in person, but he recognized the skyline and the river. He noted the docks and the tall buildings. He was on the right track. The creature adjusted his course and took the most direct route to his first target. To get the maximum amount of shock and surprise he swam underwater into New York Bay.

He swam up the bay and stayed mid-stream. He passed the Statue of Liberty then swam between Ellis Island and Governor's Island. Then he made a right turn toward the entrance to the East River. He paused over the twin tubes of the Brooklyn Battery Tunnel. He knew hundreds of humans were probably passing underneath him in their cars and vehicles. He briefly entertained the thought of crushing the tunnel while they were busily driving along on the bottom of the river and completely unaware of the danger. But he thought the better of it and continued on his way, he had more important things to do.

Opposite Brooklyn Heights he made a left turn and swam to the pier 11 area. There he stepped on land for the first time in months and headed for FDR Drive. It was an elevated roadway and presented a barrier for him. He had two choices, either smash through it or climb over it. He chose the latter and simply climbed up on the roadway and began crossing it.

Startled motorists on FDR Drive were suddenly faced with the shocking sight of a towering four legged animal in the path of their cars. There was the loud sound of screeching tires and clouds of smoke appeared as motorists slammed on their brakes. Several of the closer cars couldn't stop in time and collided with his massive front legs. He kicked them aside with the drivers still inside like the minor irritants that they were and continued on his way.

Drivers further down the road engaged in repeated rear end collisions as more and more cars were unable to stop in time. One after another they plowed into stalled cars in front of them until there was a pileup of 30 cars on the roadway. Cell phone calls began to multiply as everyone on the roadway pulled out their phones and began to call 911. They reported the accidents and a description of a 100 foot long "monster" that caused them. Emergency operators became irritated at the flood of obviously crank calls about a "monster" walking across FDR Drive causing accident pileups. Unfortunately, they couldn't ignore them because they kept hearing the same story on each call. A nearby patrol car was sent to investigate before they would send any rescue personnel.

Unaware and unconcerned about the human's problems the creature started his way down the narrow, one way strip of Wall Street in front of him. Cars were in all the lanes blocking his way. He begin to kick some aside while stepping on top of others as terrified occupants abandoned their vehicles and ran for their lives. There were screams and shouts as men and women ran in every direction trying to escape the danger headed their way. People inside buildings watched in horror and picked up phones to add their calls of distress to the suddenly overtaxed emergency calling system. So many calls were coming into the 911 system it began to overload and no more calls were getting through.

Down Wall Street he continued his trek, destroying cars along the way. He made a left turn on Broad Street and headed for his first target, the largest stock exchange in the country, the New York Stock Exchange (NYSE). The menacing animal walked to the front of the building and studied it for a moment, he sneered at its pretense. He noted its six Corinthian columns and the ornate marble sculpture, topping the façade. To him it showed the arrogance, elitism and power these people must feel about themselves. He approached the building, stood on his hind legs and tore down the marble sculpture in sections letting them smash to the pavement. He then ripped into the columns pulling them out one at a time.

Inside there was panic, most of the people inside were unaware of the unfolding events in the street. Feeling the building swaying and shaking beneath them they thought an earthquake was taking place. All of the traders and people inside began to run for the exits and out into the streets to perceived safety. But, the sight they viewed as they left the building was anything but safety. Some people were killed outright by falling debris. Many escaped none the worse for wear after the unforgettable shock of seeing a huge animal in the process of tearing apart their building.

Wherever the creature saw a window or opening he reached in and began to tear out the surrounding structure. Where there was no opening he punched one and tore out the area around it. He began to resemble some sort of gigantic anteater digging out a huge termite mound, but with masonry, stone and wood flying out instead of dirt.

With sirens wailing and lights flashing police arrived on the scene prompted by the frantic 911 calls that had gotten through the logjam. After reporting their description of what was occurring in front of their very own eyes, they grabbed their weapons and began to fire on the "monster". Their weapons had no effect; he completely ignored them and continued on with his gruesome business. Over a hundred people were trapped in the NYSE. Unable to get out they died from fallen debris and the building collapsing around them.

Leaving most of the building in ruins he was satisfied with his work. After smashing and tossing a few of the police black and white cars he left. He then headed up Broad Street to Nassau. There was more chaos as panicked drivers swerving to avoid him ran into other cars and buildings. With no way of escape they hurriedly abandoned their cars and ran in panicked flight. The creature however had no regard for them. He kicked their vehicles aside like so many toys a kid would leave on the floor.

The city and the world were waking up to what was happening. The first news helicopters had arrived and were reporting the carnage on the ground. The NYSE had been destroyed and the huge monster that did this was still roaming the streets. The local news feed was picked up by SNN and was being put on their broadcasts. The military called up its units closest to the NYC area and initiated their contingency plans for defending the U.S. homeland. It was the worst case scenario, fighting the creature in a highly populated area like New York City.

As he passed Cedar Street, then Liberty Street he turned and faced his next target, the Federal Reserve Bank also called the Fed. This bank is, in terms of assets, the largest and most important of the 12 regional banks in the Federal Reserve System. It is the place where U.S. monetary policy is implemented. It transfers trillions of dollars a day between banks. He reasoned this is a great symbol of these American's money system, so it has to come down.

He was very tempted to go after the gold in its gold vaults. The gold vaults hold more than 6000 metric tons of gold, more than Fort Knox. However they are stored 80 feet down, at least five stories below the street. It would be troublesome but not impossible for him to reach it, but what would he do with that much gold? He could of course scatter it, toss it around or crush it, but that wouldn't destroy it. Even if he could melt it the humans could still recover the gold. There is no way he can destroy that much gold easily so he decided to leave the gold alone and go after the building. Anyway the thought of digging down five stories through dirt and rubble was distasteful to him. He didn't know it but he inherited a lot of the good Dr's snobbishness.

He noted the large amount of windows in the building. There were many more windows here than in the first one. They were perfect places for reaching in with a clawed paw and pulling out walls. He ignored the occupants running from the building in streams. He had no concern for them. He didn't care if they were in the way or escaped, his only concern right now was the building. He rapidly advanced to the Fed stepping on several poor souls who couldn't get out of the way fast enough. He again stood on his hind legs and began his grim task of dismantling the building. When he stood up this way and extended his forelegs he was able to reach farther than his normal 100 foot length. He was able to reach 11 or 12 stories, almost to the roof of the building. He started his demolitions from the top down and ripped everything out sending the debris to the ground.

Helicopter gunships and F-35 fighters began to arrive, the vanguard of more forces to come. The plan called for an aerial defense. Ground troops couldn't be exposed to the extreme danger he presented. They were being moved into the area but were ordered to stay a safe distance away from the animal. The gathering F-35's were ordered to circle at higher altitudes and not attack unless the creature was in a clear area. That policy would hopefully reduce the likelihood of civilian causalities. They were to be called down by spotters on the ground or the helicopters when an opening presented itself. The jets were carrying the heaviest bombs and ground attack missiles.

The helicopters circling at lower altitudes had been given less restrictive orders. They were carrying lighter ground attack missiles and chain guns. Their orders were to attack whenever they thought the chance to kill it outweighed the risk to buildings and people. As their pilots watched in helplessness the Federal Reserve Building was being dismantled below them. They could see the ruins of the NYSE several blocks away. Who knows how many people are lying dead in those buildings they thought? The chopper pilots made their decision. Once this building was down and the deed was done they were going to try to stop him now, then no one could claim their fire destroyed the Fed. They were going to get in close to be as accurate as possible and attack. There has to be very little likelihood anyone is still alive in the Fed with tons of rubble on top of them they reasoned.

With his destructive mission on the Federal Reserve complete he turned and headed toward his next target. As he stepped away the helicopter pilots locked on their weapons and opened up with a barrage of missiles. Fire, blasts and streams of smoke filled the air as the half dozen gunships let loose their deadly cargo. At such close range most of the missiles were on target and there was a rapid chain of explosions on the creature's body. There was no reaction from him and he continued to walk on his merry way as if nothing was happening to him.

Undaunted, after their load of missiles was expended the pilots switched to their 30 mm rapid fire guns. They all fired a huge barrage of cannon shells on the animal until they expended all their ammunition. Bright twinkles of light sparkled all over his body as the cannon shells hit home. But all the fire was ineffective as the animal continued on his way with no regard for the airborne fireworks. Out of ammunition the pilots headed for home leaving one helicopter behind to shadow him and call down the jets when possible.

Turning down Liberty Street the creature advanced to the corner of Broadway and Liberty where he faced the NASDEQ stock exchange building. The NASDEQ is the second largest stock exchange in the United States and has more trading volume than any stock exchange in the world. The front of the building is covered with what was once the world's largest video display. With no concern for the people inside the huge animal began his systematic destruction of the Times Square icon. Less than twenty minutes later nothing was left of the landmark building except rubble.

The creature was tiring of this boring but necessary demolition work. However, he had only one objective left, the New York Mercantile Exchange (NYMEX) building. This building housed both the NYMEX and the New York Board of Trade (NYBOT). Ironically the NYBOT was in this building because their original headquarters were destroyed during the September 11th terrorist attacks and as a result was moved here. This move now worked to the creature's advantage because now he could kill two birds with one stone.

As he turned the corner of Broadway and Vesey Street he was momentarily stunned by the huge explosion of a white phosphorus shell (WP) directly in his face. A National Guard tank armed with these unique munitions was sitting in the middle of Vesey Street and hit him at point blank range, squarely in the face. The brightly burning shower of white phosphorus particles along with the accompanying large amount of smoke and toxic fumes temporarily disoriented him. He stepped backward from the effects of the round. The tank crew put their vehicle in reverse and quickly fired another WP round directly into his face. The creature shook his head in an attempt to clear it of the irritating properties of the WP shells. Pleased at the effect the shells were having on the animal the crew continued to rapid fire more rounds at his face and the front of his body scoring hit after hit. Stunned and temporarily disoriented the animal looked around for a quick avenue of escape, but hesitated. No, he thought, part of his mission was to prove to the humans they can't hurt him. He wouldn't give them the satisfaction of seeing him run down a side street to escape. He had to defeat head on any challenge they presented to him. He made a quick dash to the offending tank absorbing two more WP rounds in the process. The tank crew did a hasty pivot on one of its treads in an attempt to escape using its higher forward speed. But it was too late; in less than six strides the monstrous animal was upon them and began to crush the tank into so much scrap metal.

Satisfied he continued his trek down Vesey Street followed by the lone attack helicopter, several news helicopters and the circling jets overhead. He quickly passed Church Street, W. Broadway then West Street. He continued northwest until he reached his final target, the NYMEX building. He was in a hurry to finish his work in this city and tore into the building with a ferocity he didn't show at the other targets. Within twenty three minutes this building was left in shattered remains with hundreds of dead and injured trapped in the ruins.

Eager to return to the water he passed an area of old warehouses and abandoned buildings to the south. The spotter helicopter pilot noted he was heading for an area which should be sparsely populated and he was probably about to escape to the river. It was a matter of calling in the jets now or never. The circling aircraft overhead were called down and cleared to drop their deadly ordinance on the huge antagonist.

The F-35's peeled off from their perfect formations and moved in for the attack. Using their onboard lasers they locked on the animal and a barrage of one and two thousand pound laser guided bombs were released. Looking upward the creature saw a large amount of dots falling from the sky and knew this was the humans attempt at a knockout blow. He changed a little of his outside skin from matter to energy and an almost imperceptible green, yellowish glow appeared around him. There was one

163

explosion after another as most of the bombs hit their mark. Some missed the target and destroyed nearby buildings and warehouses in the process. To the amazement of the pilots he continued to leisurely walk as if none of this involved him. He carried himself in what would later be described as an almost aloof manner, almost like he was above what was happening around him. But how can you attribute human attitudes to an animal? After all he's just an animal, isn't he? These were statements about him that would be repeated many times.

From a nearby warehouse two hardened observers were watching the action through windows shattered by the concussions from repeated explosions. The men were close to the battle, almost too close. They could feel the pressure from the detonations on their bodies but continued to watch with fascination the events unfolding near them. These were men used to death, violence and killing. They were members of the criminal underworld and not people who scare easily. They were also cunning and crafty men who were always looking for an angle, a way to take advantage of any situation and make a profit.

The men were at the warehouse because it was a storage point and base of operations for many of their illegal operations like truck hijacking and theft of merchandise. As the creature passed their building he was suddenly hit by a tremendous explosion. It must have been one of the numerous bombs or rockets fired at it they later reasoned. But whatever caused it they noticed something, an object or some sort of debris flew off the thing and landed near their building. As soon as the monstrous animal left the area the two men went out to recover it. It looked heavy and was about the size of a dining room table, but when they picked it up it was amazingly light. They quickly rushed it back to the relative safety of the warehouse. They suspiciously looked around to make sure no one saw them retrieve their prize. Secure that nobody probably saw them, they examined their find at leisure under the bright warehouse lights. To their surprise it almost looked like a piece of skin. Under closer examination it didn't appear to be skin but more like a scale. It reminded them of the scale of a snake or some similar animal. This must be a piece of the animal that had caused so much damage in the city, they thought. This must be worth a lot of money, they reasoned, but how do you cash in on something like this?

With their well-known distrust and disdain for authority in mind their wheels began to turn. They figured there is no way this can be sold on the internet or the open market. The government or law enforcement would jump in and probably confiscate it. Besides, they don't want attention brought to them and too many questions asked about them and their operations. No the only way to do this is the way they always do business, below the radar and out of the public eye. They operate where you don't have to pay any taxes or have the government's prying eyes in your business. They decided this thing has to be kept under tight wraps and arrangements for sale made through their usual underworld contacts.

The creature was now at the edge of the river. Now it is time to toy with the humans and give them a hint of his next target. After all, even if they do figure out what he means what can they do about it? He waited for a pause in the din of ear shattering explosions around him. He knew his words would be heard by anyone within several blocks and reported on their news media. Again with the loudest voice he could gather he stated these words; "TO A PLACE OF DESTINY, BUT ALSO A BURDENSOME STONE. I REMOVE IT FROM YOU."

With that he entered the water and headed for the harbor entrance.

CHAPTER 19

The USS Florida was monitoring the unbelievable events in New York from its position off the harbor entrance. It was several miles out and had arrived in position too late to detect the animal's approach. Captain Hancock removed the veil of secrecy and informed his crew of their real mission which was surveillance of the creature. With the events being broadcast on all the major networks, he didn't want his crew to be the only people in the dark. Most of the crew was allowed to watch the events on the ship's TV monitors which were placed throughout the sub.

Suddenly the Florida received a flash message from headquarters. The animal had entered the water and was swimming for the harbor entrance and the open sea. Hancock read his orders and was somber. His orders were to seek out and destroy it. He was given leeway on his methods and conditions of attack but was told not to unnecessarily endanger his sub by getting too close to the animal. This last warning was something Hancock didn't need to be told. He had watched in awe the spectacle in New York. He was amazed at the strength of this thing and how much punishment it took with apparently no effect. If that thing got close to his sub it could crush his hull like an egg shell killing him and all his crew. He decided he was going to engage it at long range and not let it get close to him. His boat was in great shape and his men well trained. He had no reservations about going into combat against any enemy of the United States. However, his sub with all its capability was not designed to fight an animal. His men also had not been trained for this type of mission. Nevertheless, this thing had attacked his country, and this is a U.S. warship whose job is to defend this country. He had his orders; he was going to carry them out no matter what the consequences.

Captain Hancock reached for his microphone and broadcast to his men.

"Men this is the Captain. I know you have been watching with interest the tragic events in New York. The fly boys have had their crack at that thing, now it's our turn. I have received orders to engage and destroy that thing. The last report I have said it is heading out the harbor in mid channel and headed our way. I intend to play possum and let it pass. We're going to get between him and the coast to block him from heading back to land. Then we're going to send a few of the Mark 57 fish up his butt. Let's see if he can handle that."

The Florida moved to a position south of the harbor entrance and waited quietly. Not wanting to give away their position prior to the attack the sub left a remote probe in the anticipated path of the creature. The same type of technology used in the ocean going probes of the day had been utilized for military use, only on a lesser scale. The military probes were smaller and had a shorter endurance. They were made in versions that were small enough to be carried on submarines without sacrificing their weapons allotment. Unlike the ocean going probes they were only useful for 18 hours or so before they

168

ran out of power. They also had a limited detection range when compared with the ocean going models. However, they permitted the host sub to remain silent and undetected while receiving vital intelligence.

The creature leisurely swam out of the harbor underwater. He was tired but pleased with his work. He had accomplished all of his goals. The vaulted Americans offered him no more of a problem than the humans he faced in Ashanti. Now it was time to gorge on seafood and build up his energy. He passed the Florida's probe without noticing it. The probe was so small and maintaining station so slowly it blended in with the marine life around it.

On board the Florida the CIC was monitoring the information it was receiving from the probe. It was keeping pace with the target and shadowing it. On their monitors they were receiving an image of the beast. The initial images they got were poor because of the condition of the water and the distance between them and the probe. After some minor adjustments the subs on board computers cleared up the signals enough so the sailors could clearly see their prey. He was swimming along like he didn't have a care in the world and leisurely eating fish that came in its path. It almost looked like he was tired to the operators, a fact that they relayed to the Captain.

"So he's tired," said Captain Hancock. "Well I guess he should be after ransacking a city and killing hundreds of people. Now is a good time to give him a permanent rest. Load tubes one, two, three and four. Helm close for a long range torpedo shot but slowly, no more than a five knot closure speed. Don't spook him; I don't want him to know we're here until we let him have it."

The Florida slowly closed the distance between it and the animal, but the CIC noticed a potential problem.

"Captain, we may have a problem."

"What is it?"

"The target is picking up speed. If we increase the probe's speed much more I'm pretty sure he's going to detect it because it'll be faster than the fish around it. Then he's probably going to notice it's following him."

"Don't increase speed; I don't want him to notice it. Monitor it as long as you can, if it gets too far away from the probe track it with our passive sensors. But whatever you do, don't use the sonar. I want to keep the element of surprise."

Hancock was in his hunter killer mode. He was like a lion now, closing in on his prey. All his senses were heightened and he was ready for the kill. This thing was not going to get away from him. It had its day, in fact more than its day and nothing was going to stop him from killing it and ending its reign of terror. The submarine slowly closed the distance between it and its prey, overtaking the probe and leaving it behind. It finally lost the signal from the probe now behind it, but continued the chase using its passive sensors. There was no indication the intended target was aware they were there. It continued on its way seemingly leisurely and relaxed.

"Captain," said the CIC, "we are now at maximum range for a torpedo attack."

"Let's get a little closer," said Captain Hancock. "The closer we get the better our chances of getting a sure hit."

The Mark 57 torpedoes were the latest and most advanced torpedoes ever made. They were sometimes called the "shoot and forget" torpedoes. They were equipped with the latest in on board computers and sensors. When they were fired they independently searched out and destroyed their targets. It had never been used in combat, but in all its tests and exercises it enjoyed an almost eighty five percent success rate when fired within its design parameters.

Hancock noted they had passed the weapon's maximum range ten minutes ago. Ok, close enough, now it's time for action, he thought.

"Do we have a lock on the target with the torpedoes?" The answer was affirmative.

"Are one, two, three and four ready to fire?" The response was affirmative again.

"Fire one." There was a three second pause then he barked out "fire two."

The creature was lazily munching on what was left of a tuna when he suddenly stiffened up and became alert. Something was wrong; objects were approaching him at a high rate of speed. He turned his head quickly and saw two dots heading directly for him. They were almost upon him and they had to be some sort of weapon. He quickly dived downward with the agility of a seal. The first torpedo tried to follow him but couldn't match his almost 90 degree turn. As it passed and the distance started to increase between it and the creature, the weapon's proximity fuse detonated the warhead. The fuse registered the sudden increase in distance as a near miss and obediently ignited the warhead. This was part of its program in order to score as much damage as it could, since this was the closest it was going to get on its current trajectory. There was a huge explosion whose vibration was felt on the Florida back in the distance. A few seconds later the second torpedo, which had the luxury of being able to adjust to his new trajectory approached. He quickly made an almost 90 degree turn upward. Curving its course but unable to match his turn the second torpedo met the same fate as the first. There was a huge explosion in the distance and the Florida felt the same vibration from the detonation of its second fish.

"What happened?" said Hancock to the CIC. "Did we score a kill?"

"No, we don't think we hit him. He still seems to be swimming."

"Well why didn't we hit him?"

"The darn thing ducked our torpedoes. He turned sharper than they could and the fuses went off as they were designed to do. He's maneuvering like some kind of fish. Captain, he probably can do this all day if he wants. I don't think we have a chance of hitting him like this."

"I agree, disengage the proximity fuses on three and four, and set them for a contact hit. It looks like we're going to need a contact hit to really hurt this thing, anyway. If they miss they should come around and try again until they run out of fuel or lose their fix. Maybe they'll get lucky and hit him on one of their passes."

The torpedo men on the boat dutifully reset the two torpedoes for a contact hit and informed the Captain they were ready for firing.

"Fire three, fire four," said Captain Hancock.

The two fish rapidly streaked toward their objective. The creature, now fully alert and somewhat amused continued to swim out into the deep waters past the continental shelf. These humans actually thought they could kill me with their weapons. Even now he sensed more launches, and then saw two more objects heading toward him. He waited until the first was too close to match his turn and did another almost 90 degree turn downward. He did the same maneuver for the following object. This time they

172

didn't explode but made wide arching turns and came at him again. He easily avoided them until they ran out of fuel and both shut down then dropped to the depths below. He saw no more weapons coming so he continued on his way.

Aboard the Florida Captain Hancock had a dilemma on his hands; his torpedoes were virtually useless against something that can maneuver like a fish. Nothing man made can turn that sharply.

"Captain," came the call from the CIC. "We don't know if it will help but we noticed something during our attacks."

"Well, what is it?"

"We noticed every time a torpedo made a run on him he did a 90 degree to avoid it and the fish couldn't match his turn."

"Tell me something I don't know. I already know that."

"What we noticed was most of the time he dived downward and only once or twice did he go in another direction."

Hancock's mind began to absorb this tidbit of information. So, he is predictable, but what earthly good is that information to him? The Mark 57's are fully automatic, there is nothing he can do to program them to turn down because he thinks the target is going to turn downward. But wait a minute, he thought. He made a quick call to the torpedo room. The chief in charge answered.

"Chief do we still have any of the old Mark 48 torpedoes aboard?"

"Yeah, Captain. We left port in such a hurry we didn't have time to offload the last two."

"Do those two still have the old wire guidance capability?"

"Yes sir, they both do."

A plan was beginning to develop in Hancock's fertile mind. These last two relics of the past still possessed the old wire guidance system, which unwound a thin wire behind it as it left the submarine. The wire was used by the sub to steer the torpedo to the target. When it got close the wire was cut and the torpedo used its own sensors to hit the target. But what if they didn't cut the wire and guided it all the way to the target? Knowing it probably was going to turn downward at the last minute, they could lead the elusive animal like a duck hunter would a duck and may be able to hit him.

"Chief are they in condition to be fired?"

"No not really sir, we took the warheads and fuses off in preparation for offloading. They do still have fuel in them; we left that for the depot guys to remove."

"Do we still have the warheads and fuses on the boat?"

"No sir we offloaded them already."

"Chief, I need those fish."

"Well, the bean counters that developed the Mark 57's saved money by using the same warhead as the old Mark 48's. The fuses are different but that doesn't matter if they're set for a contact hit. If we take a warhead and fuse from a 57 I think it should work on a 48."

"That's what I want it set for, a contact hit. Do it then, I need it done ASAP. How long do you think it'll take?"

"That's kind of hard to say, we never figured on ever using the old models again so we're going to have to look them over real good. Then we have to run some system checks and also make sure the warheads fit real good. If everything goes right maybe 40 minutes but don't hold me to it."

"Chief I am going to hold you to it. We have to hit this thing before it gives us the slip. I've got the feeling he's not worried about us and that's the only reason we still have contact with him. I think if he decides he wants to get away we're going to have a hard time tracking him."

"We'll do our best Captain."

"Oh, another thing Chief, I want to use the wire guidance all the way to the target."

"They're not designed for that Captain, the wire is supposed to be cut near the target then the fish guide themselves the rest of the way, but I think we can set it up for that. However, the boat is going to have to get in a little closer than normal or we're going to run out of wire."

"Yeah, I was thinking the same thing. Let me know when you're ready."

The thought of bringing his boat and his men closer to harm's way was something he wasn't too happy about. But, this thing had attacked American soil and his job was to defend the country. He's not going to let it get away and get the chance to come back and do it again.

CHAPTER 20

The USS Florida continued to follow its adversary but kept a safe distance behind. After what seemed like hours Captain Hancock received a call from the torpedo room, it was the Chief. Hancock looked at his watch, 41 minutes had passed.

"Well Captain we're as ready as we're going to get."

"Good work, load the fish in tubes one and two."

"Yes sir."

"Helm, start closing on him slowly like before, we don't want to alarm him."

The submarine began to shorten the distance between it and the animal. He began to notice they were closing in on him but he took no action. He continued to swim, chomp on fish and keep one wary eye on them.

"Ok helm close enough, maintain this distance."

The creature noticed the human craft stopped closing on him so he relaxed and paid them no attention to them for now. He was running into more fish now and had more important things to do like replenishing his energy level.

"Are tubes one and two ready to fire?"

"Yes sir," sounded the reply.

176

"Remember now, these fish are to be guided manually until contact. We have to have a contact hit to hurt this thing. And remember he's probably going to dive straight down to avoid it. That seems to be his pattern. We have to anticipate his dive and aim where we think he's going."

"Yes sir."

"Ok here go we go. Fire one," said Hancock, then a few seconds later, "fire two."

The two torpedoes lurched from the bow of the Florida and raced ahead. In the distance the adversary became alert; the humans were trying the same thing again. As before he waited until the weapons were close before acting. A split second before they impacted he dove so they would miss. But to his surprise as he dove down the objects changed course and also headed down. Before he could react they were upon him. He was able to twist and avoid the first, but the second hit him squarely in his midsection. There was a gigantic explosion and he was driven sideways in the water.

On board the Florida the concussion was felt by all the crew.

"We got him," said the XO to Captain Hancock.

"I'm not so sure Marv," said Hancock. "CIC, what's it look like."

"He's stopped moving sir; the fish may have got him."

The creature was irritated and angry and his mind became filled with thoughts. These humans are much more ingenious and pesky than I thought. If you leave them alone their ability to scheme and plan devious plots has no end. Somehow they figured out a way to hit me and I can't figure out how they did it. I'm going to have to remember that in the future. But one thing is for sure, I can't let them sit back there and attack me anytime they feel like it. He was still low on energy from his days work in New York City and hadn't eaten enough to replenish himself. But, it shouldn't take much to smash the human undersea vessel and be on my way, he thought. He turned around and swan toward the submarine.

"Captain," said the CIC, "he's on the move again and he's heading straight for us."

"Helm make a 180 degree turn, ahead full."

Hancock knew it was no time to be a hero. He and his men had given their best shot. The thing wasn't even hurt and he had nothing left with which to fight. It's time to run and save his ship.

"CIC what's the targets status?" said the Captain.

"Sir the target is closing on us."

"Helm are we at full speed?"

"Yes sir."

"Engine room I need everything you can give me. We can't allow the target to make contact with us."

"Sir, we're running at 100 percent rpm now."

"CIC, how are we doing?"

"The target's still closing sir."

"Engine room push it up to 110 percent."

"Captain I wouldn't recommend that, if we hold that too long we're going to damage something."

"That's the least of our worries if that thing catches up with us. The sub can always be repaired but not if it's sent to the bottom of the ocean with us in it, give me 110 percent."

"Yes sir."

The Florida's hull creaked and groaned as it passed the top speed it was designed to travel. Strange noises were heard throughout the boat as metal structures which had never moved before began to flex and shift in response to the unaccustomed high speed.

"What's our status helm?" said Hancock.

"We show 110 percent rotation sir."

"CIC, what's our status in relation to the target?"

"He's not gaining on us sir, but we're not losing him either. The target is keeping up with us."

Captain Hancock couldn't believe what was happening. An animal was keeping up with a nuclear sub. How can something as big as that keep up with us? And we're at a pace to burn out our bearings and who knows what just to hold him off. But he is willing to burn out everything on the boat before he will let that freak touch his sub.

The creature was tiring. Not tiring in the sense you or I would tire but he could tell his energy level was getting low. He hadn't replenished his energy before his encounter with these humans. He wasn't able to catch them quickly and was rapidly running out of steam. Even though he would like nothing better than smash his irritants he couldn't afford to keep up this pace. After 10 minutes of high speed chasing he finally gave up the pursuit.

"Captain," said the CIC, "he's turned around and is heading east again. He's stopped chasing us."

"Helm reduce speed to slow, turn around and shadow him. Match his speed and keep the maximum separation from him we can hold and still get a good fix. We're going to track this thing. Patch our sensors directly into the Grid."

The Grid was the nickname for an advanced information, intelligence, and surveillance system with which data could be shared in real time. It had been online now for several years since its adoption in the year 2020. Any military unit or command which had the right equipment could receive it. If you had access to the grid you would be seeing the same data the Florida was seeing from their sensors about the target, including current position reports. The Florida was now the eyes and ears for the entire world in regard to keeping track of this menace.

"The menace" noticed when he turned around the human vessel turned around and began to follow him. He had decided to let them go because he didn't want to waste energy chasing them. However, it is an entirely different thing to allow them to stay on my tail and follow me, he reasoned. They probably are going to be reporting my position to others so they can plan some sort of trap. The creature reasoned they were over deep waters now; much deeper waters than the human craft can descend into and survive. So he tilted his body and dived downward.

"Captain, he's headed down," reported the CIC.

"Stay with him helm," said Hancock.

Deeper and deeper into the murky depths dove the creature with the Florida following at a respectable distance. They passed the lower limit of where submarines normally operate in peacetime and kept descending.

"Captain," said the helmsman, we're approaching 1,600 feet. That's our test depth."

"CIC, what's he doing?" said Hancock.

"He's still diving," sounded the reply from the CIC.

"Then continue your dive, stay with him."

Things keep getting more serious, thought Hancock. I guess this is where we earn our pay.

This class of sub had never been tested below its peacetime test depth of 1600 feet at least not officially. Every foot traveled below that would be breaking new ground for this class of sub. There were rumors of unauthorized forays below test depth but none that anyone would admit. However, this was a combat situation now and all the bets and limits were off.

The huge animal and his pursuer passed the imaginary line that indicated the sub's test depth limit and continued downward.

"Captain, we're at 1,700 feet and still diving," said the XO.

The XO was starting to become concerned or as he would put it, more sharply focused. He had moved over to the helmsman's position and stood behind him watching his readout.

"Shallow our dive a little helm, bring it up 10 degrees," said Hancock.

"Yes sir."

"CIC what's the target doing?"

"He's still diving and hasn't let up, he's at 2800 feet."

How deep is he going to dive, thought Hancock?

"Captain we're coming up on 1800 feet," said the XO.

The XO fixed his eyes on the Captain. He wanted to say what he was thinking about this dive. He didn't think it was wise, the target could continue to dive for who knows how long. He probably could out dive them. Maybe its plan was to draw them down below their crush depth and destroy them. After all the crush depth of any sub is never proven until it actually happens. It really is an educated estimate from computer models and engineering formulas. In reality it could be more or less than the official number. He wanted to say all this to Captain Hancock but he didn't want to question his judgment

181

in front of the crew. He continued to fix his gaze on Hancock waiting to protest if he didn't soon stop their dangerous dive.

"Helm, level us off at 1850 feet and match his forward progress," said Hancock.

There was a sign of relief from the XO. He and the Captain must be on the same page. He didn't have to say anything.

"What's the targets status?" said Hancock to his CIC.

"He's still diving sir, he's passing 3000 feet."

Captain Hancock was amazed at the animal's behavior.

"Go active on all our sonar; he knows we're here so there's no need to be quite anymore. And deploy the towed array; we can't afford to lose contact. He could go in any direction then and shake us." If he shakes us it would have the tactical advantage of attacking us from below sight unseen, thought Hancock, but he kept that thought to himself.

"Captain," said the CIC, "everything's out and pinging but our return is getting weak and scattered. We're probably going to lose him if he keeps diving at this rate."

"Launch one of our probes down to his level and keep track of him."

"Captain, there're not really designed for that depth, we don't know if they'll operate that deep. And even if they do work at that depth we can't say how long they'll last before they go out."

"Do it anyway; maybe we'll get some useful information from it."

The Florida launched one of its probes down to the 3,400 foot level, but the creature was down to 4,000 feet by then.

"Captain we lost contact with our onboard

sonar and the towed array but we have him with the probe," reported the CIC.

"Secure the towed array and stop pinging with our sonar. If we aren't picking him up it's no sense giving away our position to him. It's up to the probe now. What's he doing?"

"He's still diving and headed east, down to 5000 feet now."

Hancock was astounded. What kind of animal is this? He's amphibious; he can walk on land and breathe air, but can still dive in excess of 5,000 feet like it's nothing. How do you fight something like that?

"Captain," said the CIC, "we just lost all our signals from the probe. It probably couldn't take the pressure down there. It went out at 3,800."

"Well, keep trying; maybe we can luck up and get something."

"Yes sir."

Who was he kidding, thought Hancock? He only had two probes and he had used both of them. This thing is smart, too smart, he isn't going to do something stupid like blunder up high enough for us to pick him up or give away his position. It's the weirdest thing he ever experienced in all his years at sea. Almost all animals can be recognized by some type of noise that can easily be picked up. Why even shrimp make noise that can be detected on hydrophones. But this thing doesn't make any sound at all, at least none that can be picked up.

"CIC do you have anything on our passive sensors?"

"No sir."

"Then disconnect from the grid, we're getting out of here. Helm, bring us up to 800 feet and take a course back to our patrol position off New York

183

harbor, ahead one third. CIC, keep on the lookout for the target in case he tries to backtrack and attack us from the rear."

The creature had left his latest antagonist, the troublesome human submarine far behind him. He wasn't sure where he was going next because he was being drawn largely by instinct now. He didn't have his next target fixed in his mind like before but he knew he was done with this part of the world. Now an ancient force even stronger than himself was pulling him to a spot in the cold turbulent North Atlantic. What was there he wasn't sure, but the pull was too strong for him to resist. He had to go there and nothing was going to stop him from reaching that spot.

CHAPTER 21

Hours earlier Elisha Washington and all her coworkers in the SNN Atlanta headquarters watched in awe the destruction and carnage in New York. Leesh had gained some notoriety from her spur of the moment reporting on this same creature in Ashanti. The executives at the network had given her good marks for her impromptu reporting. They felt she had learned enough in the boondocks and she was brought back to the states to learn the workings of the larger news world. Anyway, since most of the news world saw her broadcast she was no longer a secret. Now that many people in the field knew who she was there was no reason to keep her incognito.

Leesh was transfixed while watching the monitor. This must have been what I got a glimpse of in Africa, she thought. It was the first time she had clearly seen him and he was huge. She was amazed at the power and the size of it. Nothing seemed to hurt him and he showed no fear. It gave off an air of almost indifference to the attempts humans made to kill him. It reminded her of nature shots of bears raiding bee hives for honey. The bees would swarm and attack the bear from all sides, but the bear would ignore them and continue to rip the hive and eat the honey as if the bees weren't even there.

"Hey Leesh," she was interrupted in her fixation

on the screen by a voice she knew all too well.

It was Jimmy, a particularly irritating young man in her office who for some reason had attached himself to her. There always seems to be at least one in every organization who has the annoying tendency to say whatever they are thinking, no matter how crazy it sounds.

"What Jimmy?"

"It looks like your friend is causing a lot of trouble."

"He's not my friend and I wouldn't call this trouble, I would call it a tragedy."

"Hey Leesh, I think he's following you, he must like you."

Her temper flared at the absurd and ridicules statement that came out of Jimmy's mouth. She turned and stared at the crazy, toothy grin on his face that she had grown to dread over the last few months. She started to lash out at him but caught herself. She entertained his idea for a moment. She went to Ashanti and it showed up there, she came back to the states and it showed up here. Could there be any validity to his outrageous statement? Of course not, it was just Jimmy and more of his silly rants, she concluded. Her angry moment having been brought under control she responded to her antagonist as calmly as she could manage.

"Jimmy stop being silly, a lot of people are dying out there. This is not the time for jokes."

Amazingly the smile went away from his face and he actually became quiet. Well what do you know; he does have a serious side. Well I guess everyone does, especially at a time such as this, even Jimmy.

The executives at SNN were upset. This was becoming the story of the century, maybe of all centuries and they were not happy with their coverage of the monumental events. Obviously the events in Africa and now the U.S. were somehow connected and here they were the supreme news network on the planet but were not leading the coverage. In Africa, they lucked up and got partial coverage in the port and oil fields because an almost rookie reporter showed some initiative and took a helicopter out to the location.

Most of the scenes viewed on TV were from the local channels. Once again in New York they were surprised and the local media again was responsible for most of the video. They were forced in both cases to have their blasted logos in the corner of the screen in order to broadcast their video on SNN. They concluded this was totally unacceptable; SNN is the leader in the news field not the follower. This news network has to be the first and best all the time, the executives argued. We have to be ready the next time was the consensus. They also agreed they had to find a way to make this story their own with live worldwide coverage at the next occurrence. And they were sure there was going to be another occurrence.

With all of these facts in mind the network formed a task force to pick the most likely next target and identify people and assets to send to those areas in advance of an attack. The idea was to be positioned in advance and provide live coverage to the world, thereby cementing their status as the number one news network without question.

Leesh along with the other reporters at SNN was anxious to get one of the choice correspondent spots for the "monster" coverage. It was not a very well-kept secret what the network was planning and just about everyone heard something about it. Rumors were flying wild even though many of them were erroneous. Not knowing what the actual plans were everyone was coming up with their own theories. One theory that had the most traction was there were ten locations in ten different countries that had been identified as the most likely target. That would mean there were 10 correspondent spots available and the same number of support teams and camera crews required.

Everyone began to critique their chances of getting on one of the teams and Leesh was no exception. Leesh realistically didn't feel she was seriously in the running. At best she felt she was respected at the network for her Ashanti coverage and her dedication and hard work. She also knew many people felt she just lucked into the Ashanti story. They also felt there were too many people ahead of her with much more experience and seniority that deserved a correspondent spot. While it's true she broke the story initially she wondered how much that would really count in her favor. But she just had to get in on this story, somehow. First she has to get one of the coveted correspondent spots which is a task in itself, and then she has to figure out a way to finagle her way to the next place the creature is going to show up. However, nobody has any idea where he's going next. How is she going to figure out what the brightest brains in the world can't predict?

Her thoughts suddenly went to Pastor Warren. I wonder if he can help me with this, she thought. She knew the Pastor had an uncanny ability to tap into knowledge greater than that of any man, the wisdom of the Kingdom of God. Yes, she will contact him on this matter and seek his advice.

Several days after the New York attack, the Israeli Prime Minister was pondering the decision he made a few hours earlier. Ben-Gurion was not the type of man to second guess himself once he made a decision, but this one could have a serious effect on their relations with the United States. A few days ago came the coded message from their Washington embassy. There was word that individuals in New York had obtained a scale from the creature.

Israel like most countries has a large intelligence gathering ability which is coordinated out of their embassies scattered throughout the world. Most of the world's governments have people assigned to their embassies whose sole job is to gather intelligence, Israel was no exception. In this case one of their intelligence people had a liaison in New York who had access to organized crime figures in the New York and New Jersey area. This liaison was able to give them valuable heads up information over the years that were often in advance of official sources. But this time the intelligence from him was shocking; these criminals claimed they had something almost unthinkable. They claimed they had an actual piece of the monster. They know it has some value and are making arrangements to sell it on some sort of underground auction. However, the Israeli's sources say they don't really know what to do with it.

The Prime Minister had a bad taste in his mouth at the idea of having to deal with such people, but if they were telling the truth he might have to for the sake of his country's security. Do these people realize how much this thing is really worth? This scale, if they really have it is priceless; they could ask almost any price for it.

The source said there is one advantage for Israel and a problem for the crime figures. They have a deep dislike for the current U.S. government because of its crackdown on its operations, so they don't want them involved in any of this. In fact they want this done quickly and quietly before the Feds can find out about it. So they want it done quickly and quietly, that's good.

But first there is the question about price and authenticity of the object. He was amazed that the source reported back that they were going to ask for only two million U.S. dollars for the item. So it was true, they don't know what the object is really worth.

That meant it was time to move fast, before they got wise or someone else got it first. The crafty Prime Minister called upon his old trading skills. He wanted it badly but he knew if you looked too eager or overbid in order to get an item quickly, the seller would catch on and raise the price. They were asking two million so he gave instructions to offer one and a half million with the authority to go as high as it took to get the scale. But before any offers were made the object had to be examined by one of the biologists they used from time to time. They had to have assurances it wasn't a fake.

After the longest twenty four hour period he could remember word was received on the results of the secret operation. The scientist confirmed the item seemed to be real although he had never seen anything quite like it. The agent offered one and a half million and the owners countered with one and three quarter million. So the agent agreed to their counter offer and bought it for one and three quarter million. If it were him, Ben-Gurion would have haggled more instead of agreeing to their first counter so quickly; but no harm, no foul. The most important thing was they had an agreement to buy the item.

After hasty arrangements and exchanges of frantic coded messages between their Washington embassy, the New York consulate and government agencies, the money was delivered in cash to the underworld types and the item was secured. Within hours the scale was on an El Al cargo jet on its way back to Israel.

Now the only thing that has to be dealt with is the American reaction when they find out about this operation, thought the Prime Minister. It may take a while but eventually they're going to find out about the whole episode. How much it affects our relations is anybody's guess but I'm sure I won't be invited to the White House for a while after they find out. Maybe I can smooth things over with them if I share any intelligence we get from studying the scale.

There was a fire storm of reaction in the United States after the New York attack. The press and the public began to ask the question what did the government know and when did it know it? The White House gave the previously agreed upon cover story but the press quickly tore huge holes in it. The press and politicians from both parties began the blame game, accusing more and more people and agencies of being the one at fault for the whole affair.

Gun sales hit an all-time high especially sales of high powered rifles. In spite of the fact that bullets had no effect on the creature, Americans were buying huge quantities of any high powered weapon they could find.

The disaster struck at the heart of the U.S. financial system. Most of the physical damage was to buildings and equipment such as computers. While initial trading was interrupted, backup systems outside of Wall Street, put in place after the 911 terrorist attacks were activated. As a result trading resumed the next day although somewhat reduced. Many of the fatalities were traders and staff in stock and commodities firms. The loss of their experience brought an initial element of inefficiency to market operations that slowed trading but trading did continue. Even though the systems were still functional the largest effect of the disaster was mostly psychological. The stock market dropped to all-time lows partially on the feeling of uncertainty and fear that gripped the country.

There was fear everywhere, the price of gold and silver as they often do in a crisis rose to record levels. Churches all over the country were filled for services as people sort comfort and protection from something they couldn't control or understand.

President Logan was presiding over a gloomy meeting of his cabinet, military chiefs and advisors. The worse had happened. The situation they most feared had fallen upon them.

"Well gentlemen, it looks like this thing has blown up in our faces," said the President. "This administration is going to have to answer to the American public about this whole disaster. General Hartsfield, how do you assess the effectiveness of our actions against this creature?"

"Mr. President, it's hard to come to conclusions this early after an action but I would say we mounted the best defense possible under the circumstances. This thing always seems to have the element of surprise on its side. With no clear indication of his target to aid us we brought to bear the best assets we had available. I must say he has a thing for highly populated and built up areas, places where you can't use your full range of weapons. When he reached the warehouse area we got to work him over pretty good with the heavy stuff, but unfortunately the results were the same. The Florida even hit him with a torpedo and the result was still the same, no weapon we have used seems to hurt him."

"Maybe if what we've used hasn't worked it's time we try something we haven't used."

"Mr. President we or Ashanti have used just about every weapon in our arsenal and none of them have worked."

"General, no we haven't used every weapon we have at our disposal. If I'm not mistaken we still have nuclear weapons."

There was a gasp around the table. The thought that this was even under consideration was shocking to the people at the table.

"Mr. President," said General Hartsfield, "I would strongly, very strongly advise against the use of nuclear weapons. That would be a very, very serious step and it hasn't shown itself to be necessary yet."

"It hasn't shown itself to be necessary yet, well tell me something General that hasn't been tried that might work?"

"Well I can't think of anything off hand that hasn't been used except maybe napalm or a fuel air bomb, but I'm sure there are other options."

"The problem with napalm is we don't have any," said General Hampton the Air Force chief. "It's not made any more and hasn't been for at least thirty years. And the fuel air bombs we have are relics from the past. They're old and so big you have to drop them from a cargo plane. They aren't designed to hit a moving target, they were designed to use against stationary or fixed objects. It would be pretty hard to hit a moving target from the back of a cargo plane. We don't have a sighting system for that either. It would be purely push it out the back and hope."

"Mr. President, you can't be thinking of using nuclear weapons as a serious option," said Secretary of State Clarence Adams. "Remember the only country in the world that has ever used nuclear weapons is the United States. And we've taken a lot of flak for that propaganda wise over the years. As a result we have pledged to the world we would not be the first to ever use nukes again. If we unilaterally use one again we give our enemies just what they want, to paint us as a liar and a hypocrite."

"I don't care what the rest of the world thinks. That thing attacked us not them and I want it dead. Anyway I'm not talking about a big bomb; I'm talking about something small."

"Mr. President, respectfully I have to say there is no such thing as a small nuclear weapon," said Linwood Midway his science advisor. "Even the smallest nuke gives off radiation. Also, given his fondness for making his appearance in highly populated areas, the blast and radiation from even the smallest warhead would be unacceptable."

"I figured that Lin, what I'm thinking about is using a nuke away from population centers. We still have the ability to pick him up at sea, right? I'm proposing if we can locate him at sea the Navy can hit him from one of our ships before he can get away."

The Joint Chiefs at the table looked at each other then at the chairman General Hartsfield. No one wanted to be the one to have to tell the President the bad news about his idea. Finally General Hartsfield spoke up.

"Mister President, we can't do that."

"What do you mean we can't do that, why not?"

"The simple fact is we don't have any nuclear weapons on our ships."

The President was stunned.

"What are you talking about?"

"Do you remember sir the Save the Oceans

194

Treaty we signed back in 2018?"

"Yeah, I remember there was a treaty. It was signed by one of my predecessors."

"Sir, it contained a lot of initiatives to clean up and save the oceans. But it also had an amendment to make all the world's oceans nuclear free. That would have meant free of all nuclear material. It would have banned nuclear reactors for propulsion and for weapons. We held out signing it because we have to use reactors to propel our aircraft carriers and subs or they're no longer any real use to us. In addition if we gave up our ballistic missile subs or boomers it would have crippled our triad of nuclear defense which is bombers, sea borne ballistic missiles and land based ballistic missiles. This was unacceptable for us, but because every just about every country had signed or agree to sign we were in a bad position.

We agreed to sign if an exception was made that allowed us to keep our reactors for propulsion and keep the boomers, the missile subs. The down side was we had to give up carrying nukes on our other ships. As a result the only nukes we have at sea are the warheads on the boomers and there is a limit on how many we can have of them."

"So what do you propose we do General, throw spitballs at it the next time?"

"We are examining options now and are looking at different types of ordinance that may have better results."

"Yeah, right, you don't have anything do you?"

"As of yet, no Mister President."

CHAPTER 22

Elisha Washington wanted to get in on the story of the century, maybe the most important story in the last thousand years. Her prospects however were dim; she needed an edge that would secure her a place in the network's coverage. She emailed Pastor Warren to see if he was available tonight for a phone call. She needed to actually talk to him, not correspond by email. She was delighted when she received a reply from him saying he would be able to talk to her tomorrow at 8pm. Included in the message was his personal telephone number.

The next day Leesh called the Pastor promptly at eight and was relieved when he answered after two rings. After pleasantries were exchanged the Pastor in his usual direct but friendly manner went straight to the point.

"OK Leesh what's going on with you?"

Leesh was a little embarrassed because she hadn't talked to her former Pastor in months. Now, when she did get around to calling him it was to get advice that would benefit her career.

"Oh, everything is fine here Pastor. It couldn't be better."

"Leesh, I know you and I've been watching the news just like everyone else. I've been expecting this call. The only thing I'm surprised about is how long it took you to call me."

"You've been expecting me to call?"

"Yes, you want to know where the creature is most likely to strike next; am I right?"

Leesh was taken a little aback.

"Well yes, I was interested in hearing your thoughts on the subject."

Although she could only hear his voice on the phone, in her mind she could almost see him smiling on the other end of the line. Pastor Warren was well known for his sense of humor and his quick smile.

"You know Leesh the world doesn't recognize it and even if they did they would refuse to accept it, but we are in the end times."

His voice suddenly turned serious. He continued on with his response.

"The only question for the world is am I in right standing with God? And of course there is the question of how long does the world have left? Now if you are in right standing with God it really doesn't make any difference when the end comes, but that doesn't answer your question, does it?"

"Well not really Pastor."

Leesh was becoming a little embarrassed again. Her self interest in trying to get in on this story seemed so unimportant and small compared to the magnitude of the matters the Pastor was discussing.

"Do you remember the conversation we had when you were trying to decide if you should take the job you have now?" said Pastor Warren.

"Yes, I remember it well."

"I told you then that you would be involved in earth shattering events one day. I think this may be it. Don't feel bad about pursuing this story. You're supposed to be a key player in these events."

"Are you sure about that Pastor?"

"Yes I am sure. Now in answer to your question if you remember any of the teachings you had when you were under my ministry you should remember there is a book in the bible called Revelation."

Leesh smiled, the Pastor's humorous side was back.

"Yes, I remember Revelation."

"I've noticed similarities in parts of Revelation and other scriptures to events taking place in the world for several years now like the peace treaty, the dying oceans, the world feeling so secure and at ease, and then this creature shows up. In some ways it appears that prophecy is being fulfilled, but in other ways it doesn't look anything like what most Bible scholars agree will take place."

"What do you mean Pastor?"

Pastor Warren's voice turned serious again.

"This creature, this is not what we have been taught to expect in most Bible colleges. This was never supposed to be an actual animal. The beast which appeared in scripture was supposed to an evil ruler, the antichrist, not a real animal."

"Oh, I see what you mean."

"But I will say this, if world actions and events including this creature or beast's actions continue to play out in loose parallel to what the scriptures say, at some point he has to attack Jerusalem."

"Jerusalem, you think it's the next place he will attack?"

"No I'm not saying it's the next target. I'm only saying if events continue to follow scripture he has to go there. That's where the final battle between the beast and God takes place. He also referred to where he was going as a burdensome stone. In Zechariah 12:3 God says he will make Jerusalem a burdensome stone for all people. He quoted that in New York City before he left. Yes, at some point I would say he has to go there."

After more pleasantries and promises to keep in touch Leesh ended her call in a hopeful and upbeat manner. She now had the edge she wanted. After her talk with Pastor Warren she was sure she knew the creature's next target, Jerusalem. But now comes the difficult part, how can she get to report the story for the network there? She knew from the grapevine the city was not even on the list of cities to be covered. However, maybe that could work to her advantage, she thought. With no one clamoring for a correspondent position in that city, she wouldn't face any opposition for that assignment from other more senior reporters.

To accomplish her task however, a decision maker would have to put her on the short list for the prized assignments. But at her level Leesh didn't have access to anyone with that kind of pull. On the other hand she thought, maybe I do have access to someone who may be able to help. Sam Hobby her old bureau chief was one of the most senior and well thought of reporters in not just this network but throughout journalism. Sam was still cooling his heels back in Ashanti in the final few weeks before his retirement. If she asked him maybe he would be willing to use his considerable clout to put in a good word for her.

At the Atlanta headquarters of SNN, Robert Dayton had been given the task of assigning correspondents to the so called monster project. This was the unofficial name that had been given to the networks ambitious project to be the only network to provide wall to wall live coverage of the next attack of the creature. On this particular evening he and his wife Toni were enjoying dinner at home and having pleasant conversation.

"So," said Toni, "how was work today?"

"It was ok, just an average day except for one thing."

"What was that?"

"I got a call from Sam Hobby would you believe that? I haven't talked to him in years and he calls me out of the blue today."

"What did he want?"

"That's the odd thing; he called me about the "monster project." He put in a pitch for a young reporter he trained."

"Who's the reporter?"

"You know her that young woman you met at the Christmas party, Elisha Washington."

"Oh yeah, I remember her, she seemed pleasant. Wasn't she the one who was on the air in Africa?"

"Yeah, that was her. Sam actually wanted me to give her one of the correspondent spots we picked for the network's coverage."

"What did you tell him?"

"I told him it was out of the question of course. She doesn't have the experience for something like this. I have scores of people with more qualifications than her. He must be getting senile. He should have known that without me having to tell him. He sure was insistent though, he must really see something in her."

"By the way honey, how many woman correspondents do you have on this job?"

Robert became wary. He noticed the tone of his wife's voice had changed. From twenty five years of marriage he could tell she was not just asking questions but she was leading up to making some kind of point.

"I really hadn't thought much about it, maybe two."

"Maybe two, well is it two or not?"

"Yes, it's definitely two women on the list."

"So, out of the ten spots there are only two women?"

"Now wait a minute. What does that have to do with anything? Are you trying to say we pick assignments based on sex?"

"No, I'm not saying anything. I'm just asking a few questions."

She's up to something, thought Robert.

"Isn't Elisha the one who broke the story in Africa and started all the coverage that followed?"

"Yeah, she lucked up and just happened to be in the right place at the right time. She wasn't even supposed to be on the air. She was just the only reporter around that day."

"That's funny when it happened didn't I hear everyone talking about how much initiative she showed by getting the helicopter and crew together to get those great shots in Ashanti?"

"Well yeah, that was true but she could have easily wasted thousands of dollars chasing a wild unsubstantiated story. And, look how dangerous it was taking that helicopter into all that shooting."

"If I remember correctly most correspondents who covered wars and conflicts have done basically the same thing at one time in their careers. Didn't you steal that Humvee and drive through the center of town in the middle of a fire fight once, just to get your story?"

"I can see where this is going and the answer is no. I am not going to stick my neck out and have to

201

explain why I 'm putting her on the list. Why would I do that? Give me one good reason why I would do that?"

"Well dear I'm not trying to tell you what to do but coupled with the fact that you are underrepresented on this project with women reporters, the fact is when the public thinks of SNN's coverage of this thing the one face they associate with it is Elisha. I know I think of her first report from Africa whenever I see a segment about this horrible thing."

"Hum," is all that came out of Robert's mouth in response. Maybe his wife had some good points but no, they weren't good enough. He had made his decision and that was the end of that.

Toni knew when her husband stopped talking it meant he had made his mind up and there was no use nudging him any more on a subject. It was time to let it go and finish their dinner before the mood went downhill.

"Would you like to have dessert now Robert?"

"Yes, thank you," he replied.

Later that night Robert tossed and turned in fitful attempts at sleep. Every time he was able to doze off he kept seeing scenes of Elisha Washington on camera, broadcasting from some remote location. He couldn't hear what she was saying, but intertwined with the scenes of her on camera were horrifying images of the monstrous creature destroying and ravaging buildings and people. The sights, the sounds, and the blood they looked all too real. The dreams were so realistic it was like he was there in person watching them. Even though he had his air conditioning on he awoke over and over again in a cold sweat. His pillow became damp with perspiration causing him to get up and walk to his study since he

202

couldn't sleep. What's going on, he thought? In his mind he went over the shocking and disturbing images he couldn't seem to stop dreaming. He doesn't understand the reason why but somehow he has to get this woman involved in the monster project.

At 9am the next morning Leesh got a call from her supervisor. She was at her desk in the middle of lining up priorities for her workday when he told her to drop whatever she was doing and go to Robert Dayton's office. He wanted to see her for some unexplained reason. Leesh was surprised that Mr. Dayton wanted to see her. She knew he was in charge of issuing assignments for the big project in the works, but what in the world does he want with her? Sam had already told her the bad news; Mr. Dayton was not receptive to his recommendation that she be included in the coverage of the next creature attack.

Well maybe he wants to ask me questions that might prove helpful from the first appearance in Ashanti, she thought.

Ten minutes later Leesh found herself sitting in front of Robert Dayton's desk engaging in nothing more than small talk. He was talking to her about the weather, her job, her family even TV shows.

Why doesn't he just get to the point?

She could sense the questions he was asking her were meaningless. What he's doing is sizing me up, she thought. For what she didn't know but yes, she was sure he's sizing her up for some reason.

Dayton's head was swirling with thoughts. He had read her personnel file earlier that morning and by talking to her in person he could tell she was intelligent. She probably could handle the assignment. Nevertheless, the ten spots had already been picked and reporters assigned to them. Why he was driven to add an eleventh spot and use her for that one he didn't understand himself.

"Miss Washington, I'm sure you know about the network's new project to get a jump on all the competition concerning coverage of this monster."

Finally, thought Leesh, he's finally getting to the point.

"Yes, Mr. Dayton I'm aware of the project."

"I'm not sure if you know it but no less than Sam Hobby himself recommended you for the project."

"Yes he did say something to me about that."

Leesh didn't want to lie but on the other hand she didn't want to admit she had asked Sam to put in a word for her. So it was accurate to say he said something to her about it, wasn't it?

"Well, Miss Washington, after a lot of thought on the subject, I have decided to add one more location to our coverage. I'm putting you down as the reporter for that spot. Congratulations!"

Leesh's mouth dropped open, she was completely dumbfounded. Sam had told her that he rejected his advice and she wasn't even considered. Now he was giving her the spot and acting like everything was fine. What could have happened to change his mind overnight?

"Why thank you Mr. Dayton. I don't know what to say."

"Don't thank me yet. There is the problem of where to assign you. Our team selected the ten most likely locations where he would show up next. To put it bluntly we don't have any place right now where we can send you."

"Mr. Dayton, if it's ok can I see the list of ten cities."

Dayton reached for his drawer and pulled out

his computer tablet. He punched the screen with his finger a few times then handed it to Leesh. The young reporter scanned the list of cities quickly and a smile came across her face.

"I think I have a location for you Mr. Dayton that's not on your list, the city of Jerusalem."

"Jerusalem, now were in the world did you come up with that?"

Knowing he was not a man of faith Leesh felt like it was no since telling him how she really knew this. He just wouldn't understand, but he would understand a reporter not revealing her sources.

"Let's just say I have inside information from reliable sources that the creature will definitely make that city a target."

"Well does your source say when this attack is going to happen?"

"No sir he doesn't say when, just he is sure he will go there?"

"Jerusalem, I'm not sure about that city. It just doesn't fit the profile we developed from the previous appearances. They were always port cities where he could swim undetected and come out of water with complete surprise. To get to Jerusalem he would have to cross open land and walk for miles giving away all surprise. All his targets have been a country's most important assets such as its oil industry or in our case the financial system itself. In both the cases it seems to have been money or finances he was trying to destroy. I'm sure the Israelis are fond of their capital but frankly I don't see anything there important enough for him to go to Jerusalem."

"Mr. Dayton the most important thing in the entire world to the Israelis is in Jerusalem."

"What is that?"

"It's the city itself; more specifically the old city and the temple mount site where the last temple stood. There's nothing left above ground at the temple mount site but there is the portion of the wall left they call the Wailing Wall. I would say they value these ancient structures more than anything else in Israel."

"I'll give the team Jerusalem as a possible location, but I'm not promising anything."

With his last comment Dayton released Leesh back to her regular job and told her to wait for instructions that would come later. Dayton watched the young woman leave his office somewhat amused and a little annoyed at the same time.

Everybody thinks there're an expert. You would think she would be overjoyed at being picked for such a prime assignment. Oh, she seemed happy enough so that's not what's bugging me. I guess it's the idea of her coming in here and telling us where we should send her. And this inside information stuff, where would she get inside information that none of us possess? Well I picked her even though I still don't know why, Jerusalem, how ridiculous.

Then a shiver went up his spine. He began to remember in the dreams he had the night before there were shapes of buildings in the background. The images of the buildings were nondescript and nothing stood out about them that he could recognize except one thing, they were old, very old. They looked thousands of years old like buildings you would see in one of those old biblical movies. He never got a clear look at them but they definitely had the look of Middle Eastern architecture. His dream took place somewhere in the Middle East in a city with an old world section. Could this woman be on to something?

The creature had been steadily led to this stormy area of the Atlantic off the coast of Scotland. Something was there but he didn't know or understand what was there. He had the sudden urge to dive deeper. Down he went to depths so deep there was no light. Nothing could be seen down here with the naked eye. However, with his keen senses he could still detect life teeming all around him. He was nearing the bottom of the ocean now and still hadn't detected anything worth this trip to the bottom of the sea. He didn't like it down here. It was dark and cold and it took him away from his friend, sunlight. He was like a hybrid car running on batteries down here. He could do it for hours, even without eating if he wanted. But he didn't want to do that and saw no reason for being down here. As he turned and begin to head back up to more pleasant depths he noticed something. There was something at the sea bottom. He could barely sense it but something strange and at the same time somehow familiar was down there on the bottom of the sea. He closed in to investigate.

CHAPTER 23

At a top secret base in the Negev Desert urgent plans were being considered for testing the scale recovered from New York. Very few people in the country of Israel knew of the project since knowledge of it was on a need to know basis. The Prime Minister had gathered top scientists in fields such as weapons, animal behavior and anatomy. They were headed by Dr. Yuli Katz, one of the most respected and level headed scientists in the country. He was a man whose judgment he trusted. He put him in charge because he knew he could handle this mix of scientists and technicians, none of whom had ever worked together. The PM felt Dr. Katz was the man he could trust to come up with some sort of logical result from all of their different inputs.

The team was supplied with all the data and footage from the previous attacks. Much of the data was acquired from friendly sources in the U.S, government. Prime Minister Ben-Gurion was somewhat surprised when after Dr. Katz examined the data he began to ask for more people to be added to his team. The Prime Minister had already emphasized he wanted to keep the number of people involved low in order not to arouse suspicion or notice of the project. Also, the people he began to ask for were experts in electricity, solar and nuclear power generation. What does this have to do with his task? He was told to find a weapon that could penetrate the scale, that was his only job. The more people he added the greater the chance that knowledge of the project would leak out and the Prime Minister was not ready to have to deal with an angry U.S. administration right now. However, since he appointed Dr. Katz and gave him a free rein to run the project, he had to trust him to follow his instincts. He reminded Dr. Katz of the need for maximum secrecy on this project. He then told him he could have whoever he wanted, as long as they passed a security check. His team also was confined to the base and told not to communicate with the outside world except in the presence of project security agents. All cell phones and communication devices were confiscated and hard line telephones were provided for use only at designated areas.

As head of the project Dr. Katz had an interesting but daunting challenge. Initially he thought he had a simple and straightforward task. All he really felt he had to do was line up a series of weapons he determined had a chance of success and simply fire them at the scale. Since he only had this one scale to test and there were no others he had to be careful with its use. He didn't want to use too much force and destroy it completely. No, he had to determine the minimum amount of force that could be used to penetrate the scale and reach the animal beneath it. Once that was determined the force of the weapon could be raised up to whatever amount was decided upon as most desirable for a lethal kill.

Careful preparations for his tests were arranged in order to preserve his sample. Due to the urgency of their assignment the test programs were setup before all the data and video was painstakingly examined. To their surprise one of the scientists detected a very slight distortion around the animal in certain pictures, almost like a glow but barely noticeable. In most of the video it was not there, but it did seem to appear in other clips. After extensive analysis under different spectrums of light the photos clearly showed what appeared to be some sort of distortion or energy around the creature at certain times. This was not anticipated but careful study of eyewitness accounts showed several individuals had reported seeing this effect. Their accounts were completely dismissed although as unreliable or their eyes playing tricks on them. But now here was evidence that something that appeared electrical was going on around the animal, at least some of the time. How could this be possible?

He knew certain animals like electric eels can generate an electric charge with their bodies and a considerable one, up to five hundred volts for at least an hour at a time. No animal this large or highly developed has ever been shown to exhibit such behavior, however. The expertise to understand this type of dynamic was completely out of his field, that's why he called in experts in electrical generation and more animal experts to look into this. He wanted this explored before he began testing with live ammunition. His calling of additional fields into the project had been met with consternation by the Prime Minister. He didn't have any idea what the Dr. was doing and said so, but he approved the additions. Dr. Katz pacified him by saying he would brief the Israeli leader on what was going on when he had something to report. The truth was he didn't know what he was looking for himself, yet.

It seemed like everyone involved with brainstorming the distortion effect had a different theory on what caused it. These theories seemed to mirror the type of field in which they had their specialty. None of them could be proven; all of them were pure theory and some of them pretty wild, thought Katz. They were getting nowhere with this. Then at the last brainstorming session one of the most junior technicians who had never opened his mouth through all of this asked a question.

"Since we are looking at what is probably an electrical effect, why don't we just hook up some electricity to it and see what happens?"

There was scattered laughter throughout the room as several of the noted scientists were just about to start a cascade of rebuttals stating how ridicules his idea sounded. Dr. Katz lifted up his hand and stopped them before they started.

"Wait a minute, at the onset it sounds like a silly idea, but the simplicity of it intrigues me."

Here he had some of the most imminent scientists in the country all gathered together and none of them including himself, ever thought of trying this type of test. It was just too simple for them to consider, they were all too concerned with big grandiose theories and ideas they had overlooked less challenging ones.

"I think it's worth a try," said the Dr. He quickly appointed a small group to come up with the equipment and methods for testing the scale with electricity. Since AC or alternating current is such an artificial current and not produced anywhere in nature he charged the group to use only DC or direct current. After cautioning them they were to keep in mind nothing they did was to harm the only scale they had, he told them their goal was to try to reproduce the glowing distortion. Of course any other reactions noted were to be recorded and cataloged.

Two days later they were ready to proceed. The scale was securely attached to a special fixture in a very empty hanger. Electrical leads were run from it to a transformer. On it was a panel with controls for an operator to decrease and increase power. All sorts of cameras, recorders and sensors were aimed at the scale in order to record any type of change in the object.

A small group of scientists and technicians was there to observe including Dr. Katz. Many of the people there were curious onlookers and were there to see what would happen. They were relaxed about this phase of the tests. Dr. Katz however, was not relaxed. He kept thinking if something went wrong how in the world would he explain to the Prime Minister he destroyed the only sample of its kind, before he came up with an effective weapon? Katz gave instructions to proceed with the utmost caution. Every step was to be checked and double checked for any type of reaction, especially any potentially damaging reaction. The four scientists conducting the tests were given a prearranged test program to carry out. No testing on the fly was to be done, the stakes were too high.

The lead scientist nodded to Dr. Katz he was ready to proceed and the Dr. nodded back to him to start. The first tests were at low power settings, no more than would be used in a flashlight or a typical hand held battery device. No reaction was noticed so the power was steadily increased in steps. After all of the low power tests were completed the power level had reached a point where it could run a typical household light bulb, that is if it could run on DC. They reached a built in pause in the testing at this point and the scale was thoroughly examined for any damage. None was detected and Dr. Katz gave the go ahead to proceed to the next round of testing, the mid-level power tests. At this point Dr. Katz retreated to his office and let the scientists continue with their painstakingly slow and careful testing program.

After hours of applying power, stopping and examining the scale, the power level had been raised almost to the wattage used by a normal kitchen stove. No reaction had been detected as yet. At this point Katz stopped the testing program to ponder whether they should continue. No reaction so far he thought; what were they to conclude from that? It could be they hadn't used enough power so far or it could be no matter how much power they used nothing was going to happen. The power levels were getting pretty high now, high enough to kill a person or severely damage or even destroy the scale.

With no evidence of any possibility of success, Katz made the decision to cancel the remaining electrical tests. It was unacceptably risky to continue these tests with no indication there was a good chance of success. This scale was much too valuable to risk. The scale was secured and safely put away. All of the data gathered from the sensors were to be studied today and tonight to see if anything useful had been learned, from what appeared to be an unfruitful series of tests.

The next day after analyzing all their data a report was given to Dr. Katz. It showed about what he expected, there was no real change or effect noticed from the scale in reaction to the power that was applied. But there was one unforeseen discovery, the scale turned out to be one of the best conductors of electricity ever seen in an object made of solid matter. It was a much better conductor of electricity than either copper or aluminum. Its resistance level, measured in ohms, was so low it approached that found in a vacuum. Also, the energy applied to it seemed to actually show an almost imperceptible increase at its exit point. It was almost as if the energy increased itself by just passing through the scale. Of course that is impossible so the report attributed the energy increase it recorded to errors or defects in their equipment or faulty calibration.

Now it was time to proceed with the main purpose for which they were there. An effective weapon that could penetrate the scale had to be found. The weapons tests on the object with live ammunition started out as expected. The first tests were with small arms such as rifle fire and machine guns just to see if it still had its armor like qualities. After all it was not on a living animal anymore but was in a fixture separated from its body.

What they didn't know was by virtue of them doing their live fire tests outdoors in the relentless desert sunlight they were increasing the strength of the scale to almost normal levels. As a result the small arms fire had no effect on it but ricocheted off it harmlessly. A deliberate but steady increase in the power of the weapons being tested was in order. Again keeping in mind not to waste time and energy testing weapons that already were found ineffective, tests were conducted from a previously prepared list of new candidates.

Weeks later after going through their lists of armor piercing rockets, tank and artillery shells they had exhausted their test candidates. All their choices failed. Nothing was able to pierce the armored scale.

Prime Minister Ben-Gurion was in a very pensive mood. He also felt very humble and powerless. He had been sure the scientists would come up with a solution that would defend the country from what he sensed was a date with the horror, which was ravaging the world. In his mind he is sure the creature is coming here and also he feels he knows its target. After going through their entire prepared checklists however, the scientists could still find no effective weapon. They were left to try experimental weapons and weapons under development, but not operational as yet. These were weapons that showed promise but were not ready for use. He didn't have much confidence any of them would work any better than the operational weapons already tested.

He began to think about something that had concerned him for a long time, the lack of dependence on God in their modern society. Ben-Gurion had grown up in a very religious household and in his youth held on to his families religious beliefs. Although in his adult years, the trials of life, also the cruelties and chaos he witnessed and participated in during years of war hardened him. He like a lot of the country had become so focused on battling the enemies all around them, they had developed an attitude of self-reliance and a can do spirit. This gradually progressed into a self confidence that they could accomplish almost anything by themselves without help from anyone. They had done this so long that they had begun to include the need for God's help as something they could also do without. We hadn't actually said that but somehow the thought must have crept in, reasoned the PM.

The modern day Israelis wouldn't come out and say something that sounded so arrogant. After all, we're still proud of the fact that most of us were born Abraham's seed and an inheritor of the promise

God made to Abraham. On the other hand our deeds and actions in everyday life show how we really feel. The sad truth is after all our history and connection to God we have become a mostly secular state. Why even our enemies pray more to their God than we do to our God. Also he hated to admit it, but even people who worship false Gods and idols pray more to them than God's chosen people do to him. Now that's a term you don't hear much anymore, God's chosen people.

He laughed at himself, he was starting to sound and think old. He was starting to sound like his parents. The situation the country finds itself in is no laughing matter, however. Nothing men have tried has resolved this problem. If something isn't done soon man may lose his dominant position on this planet and become secondary to an animal. The very thought of this is unthinkable.

However, as the Prime Minister of Israel his first thought and duty is to Israel. We don't have any defense against this with our modern weapons. What else can we do?

As he became older he looked with sadness at how most of our modern society had abandoned any pretense of the religious values of their past. There is no reliance on God in our present day society. Now we face a horrible threat for which we have no defense.

Maybe it's time for us to go back to God and ask him to help us. No its not maybe, I can't see any other way it can be done. But I am the Prime Minister and only a politician. How in the world can I get the country to make such a major change? I have no control over what people say or think, but there is one thing I can control. The military will follow my orders no matter how they think, and as the operating head of the government I can influence people. If there is no answer for this in the present, maybe there is a solution for this in our past.

A plan was beginning to develop in his mind. He picked up his phone and began to make calls. I may lose my office for this but I'm not going to just sit by and do nothing.

CHAPTER 24

Prime Minister Daniel Ben-Gurion had known Rabbi Isaac Peled for over fifty years. He had chosen a different path than him, but in his chosen profession he had been as successful as the Prime Minister. In many ways he had been more successful thought Ben-Gurion. He never had to kill anybody to serve his country like I had to do. He was his perfect choice for a big job he had in mind. When Ben-Gurion called him and asked for a meeting the Rabbi agreed to come to his office. Three days later the two men met in the Prime Minister's office.

"I called you here old friend because our country is in grave danger and I need your help," said the Prime Minister.

"Why of course, you can count on me for any assistance I can give you. What is the problem? Does it have anything to do with this abominable creature that is cursing the world right now?"

"Yes my friend, I'm afraid he is the problem. I'm almost sure he's coming here."

"Coming here, why would he come here? We're such a small country and he has the whole world from which to pick. He probably doesn't even know we exist. By all rights we should be passed over and not even affected by this."

"You would think that wouldn't you? But our

history has shown we never get a pass on anything. Look at our ancient history. Look at all the people we had to fight since God brought us out of Egypt. We have always had to fight to possess the land and then to keep it. Then we lose it and are scattered all over the world. In modern times we didn't start World War II, we weren't even a nation then, but we were the ones put in the gas chambers. The American's attack Iraq and we are the ones who are attacked with scud missiles. And every one of these Middle Eastern countries that attempt to get nuclear weapons use us as the reason they want them, to wipe us off the face of the earth. No, I don't expect us to get a pass on anything."

"Yes, all you have said is true."

"But there is something the public doesn't know. I ask you to keep this information in extreme confidence."

"Yes, I will not tell anyone."

"We have a top secret project to find a defense for this creature. We have acquired an actual scale from the animal and have been running weapons tests on it. In spite of this, we have had nothing to show for the effort but failure. Nothing we have works on this thing. We had no more success than the rest of the world."

"My God, if he comes here then what are you going to do?"

"Well, that's where you come in Rabbi. I've been doing a lot of praying and meditating on this. I know from our conversations in the past, you share my concern with the way our nation has drifted into a more secular society over time. Maybe that's why we've had so much trouble over the years. Although do you remember how in the scriptures God said, if we return to him he would help us and heal the land?"

"Yes Daniel I am well aware of what the scriptures say."

"Forgive me Rabbi; I wasn't trying to be condescending to you. Please don't take this personally."

"I don't, please continue Daniel."

"The point I'm trying to make is everything man has tried doesn't work on this thing. Maybe it's time we turn to God and ask for his deliverance. I feel we need to do this individually and as a nation."

"I agree; this is a very commendable goal. But tell me, Daniel, how are you going to do this?"

"It's not me that's going to do this. Oh, I'll give as much assistance as I can and offer the full backing of my office to this effort. But you my friend are the one who is going to do it."

"Me, do you realize how much division there is in our country among the different religious sects? And there are so many people who don't even see a need for God anymore. They don't even see a reason to change; I think you picked the wrong man for this job. You need to ask somebody else."

"No, I picked the right man alright. You may not realize it but I've talked to many people and you are one of the most respected clergyman in the country. When you talk people listen to you, even if they don't agree with you they listen. And, if they listen there is always a chance they will act on what they hear. My staff will work with you and are already working up a series of meeting with you and other religious leaders. I want you to get as many people as possible repenting and praying for our deliverance from this creature. If you need TV time or any other help let me know. I can't stress how important this is to our very survival."

"Do you really think it's that serious?"

"Yes I'm afraid so, I think this animal is intelligent and he has more on his mind than just random destruction. I feel he wants to control the world and what we see now is just a preliminary to what he has for us in the future."

"As long as you put it that way I don't see how I can refuse. I'll do my best."

"By the way there is one more thing I want from you."

"What's that Daniel?"

"I'm still not convinced there is no weapon that can work on this thing."

"But I thought you said you tried everything?"

"That's true; we or the other countries tried just about every modern weapon on this thing. But if I remember correctly as a hobby you have educated yourself into becoming one of the most knowledgeable experts on ancient weapons used during the kingdom period."

"How in the world can that be of any use to us now? Even troops armed with slingshots and stones were a valuable part of the army during that period."

"I'm not discounting anything. I want you to give me a list of every weapon used by the army during that period. Leave nothing out no matter how unimportant it looks to you. Do you think I can have it tomorrow?"

"Yes, I can have it for you tomorrow."

"Thank you I really appreciate your help?"

The two men rose from their chairs and shook hands then hugged. As the Prime Minister escorted him to the door the Rabbi asked a question.

"Oh, by the way do you have any idea where he will go if he comes here?"

Ben-Gurion looked at his old friend. He had forgotten to mention that bit of information.

"Why Jerusalem of course."

Dr. Yuli Katz studied the crazy list of ancient weapons the Prime Minister had sent to him. Some of them were so foreign to him he had to look them up to even understand what they were. Some of them like slingshots and catapults were laughable. He started to toss the list into the trash but something restrained him. After all his people hadn't come up with anything and he had the best weapons people in the country. He might as well look through the list instead of throwing it in the trash can.

Just as he thought, after he looked at them all he saw nothing that appeared useful. However, there was one item that intrigued him. There was one weapon on the list that was called darts. What in the world was a dart? He had never heard of a dart as a military weapon. His research of the word dart revealed it was a short spear or smaller weapon that was thrown at a target by hand. No pictures were available so the only darts he had an image of were in the game where you throw them at a board placed on the wall.

He thought of the darts he played with as a child. They were small with feathers on one end. The business end came to a point which embedded itself into the dart board when thrown. He remembered they were finally taken off the market because of safety concerns. That pointed end was just too dangerous if you hit something other than the target, like people or animals. Yes, too dangerous, he thought. The end of a pointed object like that must transmit a tremendous amount of force to such a small area. Of course the limiting factors would be how fast you could accelerate it and the tendency of the point to bend or break on impact if the force was too high or the target too hard.

Extensive research by his team determined the weapon of old could be anything from a short spear to a seven or ten cm length projectile similar to the dart of the Dr.'s childhood. After examining several different designs the team decided the best candidate on which to concentrate its testing was a small dart only five cm long. If it could be accelerated to the speed of a 7.62 mm bullet or faster at the pointed end it would develop a tremendous force on impact. To cut down the chance of the likely failure of the pointed end, it was shortened as compared to the childhood dart. What the technicians wound up with was what looked like a 20 mm round with a peculiar dart shaped head.

When the round was fired in tests against targets huge blunt force effects were recorded. But as predicted, when tested against the actual scale it failed to penetrate. The small pointed end flattened or bent under the enormous pressure of all that force on such a small area. The point just wasn't hard enough to handle the excessive forces it encountered. It had to be hardened somehow. One of the scientists said why not harden the point and the whole projectile? In addition he suggested several options for accomplishing this hardening. After examination of several different proposals a depleted uranium and titanium alloy was picked as the best candidate. The projectile was going to be made of one of the densest metal alloys known to man.

Fifteen days later, after around-the-clock preparations, the scientists and technicians wheeled out the components of what they hoped would be the solution to their problem. The fixture with the scale attached was positioned on the firing range along with a weapon chambered for the round they had developed. If this didn't work they were out of ideas. Six special rounds fabricated with the exotic alloy had been prepared and were ready to be fired. After careful alignment of the weapon and all the cameras and recording instruments were set up, they were ready to proceed. The first test shot was set for a distance of 91 meters or 300 ft.

From his observation post several meters from the test Dr. Katz looked at his watch and noted the time. It was near 12pm, high noon he thought. That's what it was called in the old cowboy movies he used to watch as a child. How appropriate, that was the time for many of the climatic gun fights in those old movies. And, now high noon is their moment of truth.

The head technician supervising the test signaled to Katz, everything was ready. Katz gave the signal to proceed. There was a loud report as the gun was fired and the dart shaped projectile raced to the target. Looking through his binoculars Katz could have sworn he saw something fly off the scale. But it could have just as easily been his imagination or the round itself shattering as did so many of the other munitions. In an uncharacteristic show of emotion most of the technicians conducting the tests ran to the target to get a look at the results. From his position Katz saw a lot of pointing, excitement and laughter from the men and women surrounding the fixture. He picked up his portable radio.

"What's going on down there, he demanded in a slightly irritated tone? Somebody tell me something."

"It worked Dr.," came the reply from one of the men standing around the scale. "It went through the scale."

The voice on the radio didn't identify himself in all the excitement, but it sounded like one of the younger technicians he only remembered as Samuel. The Dr. was never big at remembering last names but he did remember first names. Katz understood their excitement, he was feeling it also. He had to see it for himself. He jumped into his golf cart and drove to the target to get a firsthand look at the results.

When he pulled up beside the fixture all of the smiling scientists staring at him parted like the Red Sea and opened a path for him, allowing him to walk unobstructed to the scale. All the noise and chatter had stopped. It was suddenly so quite you could hear a pin drop as he walked to the scale. And there it was; a neat hole was there in the scale where the dart shaped round went through it. It was the first time they had seen anything penetrate it. This was monumental. A range of emotions went through Katz as different voices all began to talk to him at the same time.

"It worked Dr. isn't this great?"

"Congratulations, Dr. you did it."

"We did it Dr. aren't you pleased?"

Dr. Katz let them continue for a few moments then stopped them.

"Ok, that's enough congratulations for now. Let's get back to work. We have to continue with the test program and find out the effective range of the shell. Everybody get back to work and reposition the equipment for the next shot."

There was still much work to be done. The new munitions worked at 91 meters but it would be pure suicide to stand that close to the beast to get a shot at him. And, there were the other issues which dampened his enthusiasm. He had discussed those issues with very few people, but because of these issues they wondered along with him if any test they conducted would have any meaning.

225

They continued with their live fire tests by moving the scale backward in 91 meter increments then firing at the target again. After several cycles of this they discovered the max distance they could achieve penetration was at 500 meters or 1641 feet. Any distance greater than that and the round simply bounced off. They had their range; if a gunner could get within 500 meters of the beast he had a chance to be effective.

Later that night Dr. Katz called Prime Minister Ben-Gurion.

"Mr. Prime Minister I am pleased to inform you that we apparently have achieved success with the new weapon."

"Wonderful Yuli, this is great news. Congratulations to you and your team."

"Thank you sir."

"But Yuli, you don't sound very happy about it. I noticed you said that you apparently have achieved success. Did your shots go through the scale or not?"

"Yes sir, we put several holes in it, so many in fact that we can't use it anymore. Its structural integrity has been compromised."

"Well what is this hesitancy I detect in your voice? Come on spit it out, what's wrong?"

"Nothing's really wrong; it did what we wanted. It's just that there are other unknown issues which worry me."

"What issues?"

"Well there are several unknowns. First this scale was on what looks like a living creature that moves, but we put it in a stationary fixture by itself and took perfectly aligned shots. In actual use the target won't be stationary but will be moving. The shots will not be perfectly aligned but will be from all different angles and few of them will be from our perfect angle. Also, who knows what interaction any one scale may have with the body and the other scales that may give it more resistance to damage? Then there is the fact that we have had this thing for several months now. It's bound to have deteriorated some since it came off a live animal, that's if you can call it a live animal. We just don't know how much it has deteriorated which would weaken its strength."

"I've noticed you said it looks like a living creature and if you can call it a live animal. Those are strange choses of words. What do you mean by them?"

"That's another unknown issue Prime Minister. It walks, moves and looks like an animal, but we are the only people who have had a close look at any part of it. I have to tell you the right scientists need to examine this thing more thoroughly. We didn't waste time running a lot of tests on it because our job was to test weapons and do it quickly. All I can say right now is it looks like animal tissue but to some of us it looked like an imitation of animal tissue."

"What are you saying? Just go ahead and say what's on your mind."

"I can't say anymore right now without any real evidence. It's just a feeling we have that this is the imitation of an animal instead of a real animal."

"Yuli, you're giving me a headache. Is there anything else?"

"There are just two more things that concern me."

"And pray tell, what are those?"

"In some of the video you sent to us I'm sure you noticed a very slight sort of glow around the animal at certain times."

"No I didn't watch all of them but I heard about that from others who saw it."

"We tried to reproduce the effect but we couldn't. We think this may be some sort of electrical field the animal may be able to produce for the purpose of self-defense, something like a force field. If this is true we have no idea how effective our weapon would be against it."

"You said you had one more thing," signed the Prime Minister. "Please don't come up with anymore concerns after this last one."

"Well the last one is huge Prime Minister. If all our other concerns are false and none of the other things stop us there is one unknown for which we can't account. We were able to shoot through a scale, but who is to say what's underneath that scale on the actual creature. That could be the only scale, there could be several layers one on top of another, or the scales could be overlapping. So instead of one scale we may have to pass through multiple scales just to reach the creature."

"So what you are saying is we may have wasted all this time and effort to develop something that doesn't even work."

"That's a definite possibility Mr. Prime Minister."

"Yuli, I'm going to ask you to give me some kind of odds on the chances of this weapon succeeding. I know you can't guarantee anything and I won't hold you to it, but I need to know what you feel is our chance of success."

"Sir if I had to go out on a limb I would say at best our chances are 50/50 that we will have success."

"Thank you Yuli for your candid assessment. This confirms my thoughts that we have to attack this problem in more than one way. We're going to go all out producing the weapon, while at the same time use other more powerful weapons we have ignored for too long."

"Good night Yuli, and thank you again."
"Goodnight Mr. Prime Minister."

CHAPTER 25

The world waited for the appearance of the horrible monstrous creature, but mankind has a short attendance span. It's hard for men to focus their attention too long on one thing and even this terrible nightmarish thing was no exception. After several months passed with no reappearance of the terror, most of the people in the world again turned their attention back to other things. People still had to go to work, pay bills, keep the car running, pay the mortgage, and do a dozen other things all at the same time.

However, still in the back of their minds there was the fear that this thing would show up in their town. But, most people rationalized the possibility as you would the chance of an earthquake happening in your backyard. Everyone knows one is going to happen but probably somewhere else. Another train of thought was since you can't do anything about it why worry?

Rabbi Peled had made the rounds talking to the various religious groups and their leaders. He was pushing the idea of national unity in a prayer of deliverance for the country. This would include repentance for the nation turning away from God. He had to report to the Prime Minister that he had some success but most of the religious community didn't see the need for what he was requesting. His mission was not going well and the outlook for success was bleak.

"If the leaders don't see the need maybe their people will," stated the Prime Minister. "Maybe it's time for a direct appeal to the people. If the leaders won't lead, let them follow."

Ben-Gurion scheduled a nationwide address to the people of Israel to explain the need for such action. He decided it was time to alert them to the approaching menace the likes of which their country has never faced. He felt it is such a menace that the participation of everyone in the country is needed to defeat it.

The whole story can't be told, however. The complete story about the scale and the weapon has to be kept secret for now. The situation with the U.S. is too sensitive at this point. It can't be revealed that Israel basically stole the scale from U.S. soil from right under the noses of the American government. What the country is going to be told is only that it needs to fight the coming danger by prayer and repentance.

The big beast drew closer to what attracted him on the ocean floor. He was at an extreme depth now and there was no visible light on the bottom. His keen sense's, however, detected something was there on the ocean floor. Now he was directly above the object. It was covered with sediment but he could definitely tell there was a shape underneath all that muck. He began to dig and wipe away centuries of ocean bottom. More and more of what was beneath the surface was becoming exposed. He began to work faster when he came to the realization that what was underneath was beginning to show a familiar shape. It was a shape that was the mirror image of him. The impossible was beginning to happen. He had found himself buried under the cold, deep North Atlantic. But it couldn't be him because he was standing here and that was lying there, he reasoned. So he began to think of what he sensed as it, not him. Still there it was lying before him completely inanimate. There was no movement so there was no indication that it was alive. How could this be possible? There is only one of me. I have to be one of a kind. As he studied what was completely exposed now his mind began to work overtime.

The beast could sense the figure was not dead, just inanimate. That's all dead meant to him. He was matter or energy, whichever he picked. He could also be any combination of both at his choice. The only difference between himself and the mirror image before him was it was absent of energy. He touched the torso with his right paw and sent a surge of energy through the body. He could sense the power streaming throughout the body, slowly changing its appearance. The mystery object gradually began to look more and more like the creature. It was beginning to look healthy and alive, like an animal sleeping on the ocean floor. After a few more minutes of this he stopped and examined his handy work. It appeared groggy but it was aware and its eyes were opened. Now there was no doubt that he would be victorious in his mission. Now there were two of them.

Prime Minister Ben-Gurion was pleased with the way things were falling into place. His nationwide address to the country was received with skepticism and suspicion by the press and the powerful elite.

They questioned his real motives and saw no need for change. Some even questioned his sanity and wondered aloud if he had gone mad. Others said he had overstepped his bounds and pushing religion and prayer was not his job. Most of his opposition said there was no evidence that the evil creature was coming here and saw no reason for such a drastic change in the nation's behavior. They were happy with the way things were and wanted to keep the status quo.

But, the latest opinion polls show his appeal struck a chord with a large percentage of the county. Many people had felt a disconnection from the God of their fathers. They had felt helpless and powerless in a modern society which they felt only looked at them as a number. They warmed to the idea that they could make a difference and the idea that the nation could be saved by their act of prayer and repentance. The Prime Minister asked for a daily prayer of deliverance and was pleasantly surprised to find out more and more Israelis began to actually do as he asked.

Production of the new weapon was going well, also. They were able to use existing automatic crew manned weapons because they designed the rounds to match existing munitions casings. The only real problem was producing the odd shaped exotic round. After solving initial problems with mass production of the round they were being rapidly manufactured around the clock at different locations throughout the country.

The organizing and training of specially equipped troops was going well also. They would be the country's last defense against the monster and were all armed with the special dart shaped rounds. They were all volunteers and would fight the last stand against the creature if the conventional armed forces were unable to stop the animal. To give them the best chance of survival some of their automatic weapons were mounted on fast vehicles which would enable them to fire and maneuver at the same time. It would be suicidal to ask them to stay stationary and fire at such a dangerous foe. They had to be given a reasonable chance to live through this coming battle.

The last inner ring of defenders for Jerusalem and the Wailing Wall didn't have the luxury of mobility. These were special volunteers who would stand in their positions and continue to fight until either death or victory. Because of the gravity of this, no one was assigned to this position. They had to volunteer once again to be put in the last inner ring of defense. There was no shortage of volunteers.

Yes, things were going well. In the back of Ben-Gurion's mind however, was the warning from Dr. Katz. No matter what is done there is no guarantee of success. So their ultimate reliance for victory would have to be on God.

Elisha Washington was awakened from her daydreaming by the sudden jolt of her airliner. She instinctively looked out the window at the right wing to see if anything looked wrong. Ok, the wing was still there attached to the fuselage. It must be just a rough air pocket they flew through. She looked down and through the breaks in the clouds she could see the ocean below. Her airplane was only a few hundred miles out in the long flight to Israel. She almost couldn't believe what had happened to her in just a few short years. It seemed like yesterday when she came to SNN and now she was in on one of the biggest stories of all time. She was to be the correspondent in Israel for the monster project.

The network didn't seem to believe that there was much chance the creature would come to that country, however. As a result she was given a reduced crew of two cameramen, a satellite truck and other associated equipment. Some would have taken this as an insult compared to the resources sent to the other locations. But, Leesh was happy with this limited response. The bottom line to her was she would be in the right place and have everything she needed to broadcast live. Now if only the evasive and mysterious creature would cooperate and show up before the network's support got shaky and they pulled the plug on her.

The two creatures beneath the sea had formed a close bond after the discovery of the second. Their minds and thoughts had merged and they developed a working relationship during their weeks together.

The first took a leadership role and became what you would call the alpha male in the animal world. But they were not real animals, they were artificial creatures and as such there was no male or female. Reproduction was not one of their concerns, after all in theory they could live forever. All they needed was some sort of energy like food or sunlight to replenish themselves and they could remain the dominate life force on this planet for all time. At least all that was true in theory.

The first creature became the natural leader because he was completely fearless and had never known defeat. Because of their feeling of invincibility and prospect of eternal life, they began to arrogantly give themselves names. The first begin to call himself Alpha, the second Omega. They knew after they subjugated the humans they would have to have names to be called by and it suited them to be called these names. It's better that they pick their own names than allow the humans to name them. Why should they? After all the humans will be the slaves not us.

The two began to think alike and act alike the more time they spent together. They began to hunt the sea life they encountered in a way similar to lions. Omega learned to chase and herd the fish. The more aggressive Alpha would wait silently in ambush and score the first kills as Omega closed up the rear and joined in the slaughter. Their technique was simple, kill everything they could first then leisurely dine on the floating carcasses after the survivors had fled. They became more and more efficient at this tactic and as a result the depletion level of marine life in the area doubled in comparison to when there was only Alpha. They shared the same zeal for killing and as before when there was only Alpha, after they ate their full they continued to kill for the sheer joy of it.

Alpha learned from Omega the details of its creation. Eons ago the same machine that created both of them was discovered by men of that earlier age. Where it came from nobody knew. It was considered a religious object by the ancient people of that day and could only be used or touched by the priests. Several of them died trying to use it during religious rituals but finally one priest was able to harness its power. His thought patterns and nightmares created Omega. As history repeated itself centuries later, all of the uncontrolled, destructive, impulses and desires of man was deposited in him. These were magnified and combined with unlimited power. It went on a rampage that destroyed the ancient peoples' civilization so completely there was little record left they ever existed. They are only remembered now in fables and legions much like the lost Kingdom of Atlantis. Too late the priests realized if the machine could create him it could also destroy him. The same brave priest who was able to operate the fantastic machine harnessed it one last time to send him away to the bottom of the ocean in the far, unknown North Sea. There he was cast to lay immobile in the dark, cold temperatures and crushing depths forever. The machine was deemed too dangerous to be ever used again and was buried deep in a cave. The cave was filled in and the entrance was destroyed, but centuries of erosion by wind and water finally exposed the entrance enough so that it was discovered by Dr. Peterson.

With the machine finally destroyed by Alpha after his creation there was nothing that could stop them now, they both figured. It was now time to leave the area off Scotland and move on to continue their string of victories against the feeble humans. Thinking now as one, the two creatures began their leisurely trip to their next target, Jerusalem. Now with two of them instead of one they were supremely confident. Who could stand up to them or stop them? The answer to that question had to be no one. Soon it would be time again to kill and destroy.

Leesh comfortably settled into her assignment in Jerusalem and then waited for something to happen. Every day she searched the news media for anything that might give a hint as to where the creature was headed. During her three weeks in the city there were no reports about the creature. It was as if it had disappeared from the face of the earth. He hadn't been seen anywhere and she was starting to get a little nervous. With teams positioned all over the globe she knew SNN was starting to get a little antsy about how much money the project was beginning to cost. She knew pretty soon the network would be looking for ways to cut costs. Leesh was sure she would be one of the first to go. After all her operation was just an afterthought. There wasn't much confidence in the halls of SNN that anything would come out of Jerusalem.

In the meantime she occupied her days sending reports on the curious happenings going on in Israel. Under the encouragement of Prime Minister Ben-Gurion many of the people had discovered a prayer life and a respect for the things of God. It seemed to be a growing movement that appeared to be getting larger each week. All of this seemed to be predicated by the belief among the Israelis that the creature was somehow coming to Jerusalem. The world was baffled by this development and saw no reason why they felt this way. Leesh could understand what they were feeling. She was sure they were right and if that were true they would need all the prayer they could get in, and then some.

There were also the strange and curious military movements and activities in Israel. Troops and equipment were on the move all over the country. It was an atmosphere of preparation for war in the air. Most curious of all however, were the activities around Jerusalem. All over and around the city weapons mounts were being installed. Many of the military experts said they appeared to be mounts for large caliber automatic weapons. These were the very kind of weapons that appeared to be the most ineffective against the monster.

Why waste time and effort installing weapons that don't work, she thought? Of course no weapon has worked against it so far, but why so much emphasis on one of the least powerful weapons?

Also there was the strange huge tent that was

erected in front of what was called the Wailing Wall. It actually was all that was left of one of the perimeter walls of the Second Temple. The tent looked almost as large as an aircraft hangar, anything could fit in there. Despite repeated inquiries the Israelis would not divulge what was inside, but something definitely was inside the huge tent. What actually was inside was anybody's guess.

The reports Leesh sent in to the network received scant attention in the U.S. and even less attention in the rest of the world. The world just wasn't interested in the strange activities in Israel, the world had other concerns. Most of the countries of the world which had navies had their ships out at sea searching for any sign of the creature. Most of the world's surveillance satellites also were busy scanning the globe looking for the nightmare menace. All their efforts produced no fruit, however. With no clear place to look it was like looking for a needle in a haystack once again.

CHAPTER 26

The subject of the entire world's attention was
now only a few miles off the coast of what used to be
called the Gaza Strip. It along with the West Bank
now made up the independent Palestinian homeland.
Alpha had retained much of Dr. Peterson's knowledge
of world geography, so he had a good idea of the lay
of the land in the Middle East. He knew the city of
Jerusalem wasn't a port city like his other targets. So
he and his companion couldn't achieve total surprise
by swimming right up to the city as in the past. No,
they would have to cross an open area of land to
reach the city. That means the humans would have
warning this time. But what good would their
warnings do them? After all there wasn't anything
they could do about it anyway. The human's
weapons at most only irritated them with their loud
explosions and bright flashes, but they decided to
avoid them on their approach.

They chose an area mostly devoid of people to
come ashore. They knew the Israelis' would have a
large military presence on their coast but nothing in
the Gaza Area. They also knew the Gaza territory
was demilitarized as part of the peace treaty and
there were no armed forces in the former territory.
The two intelligent creatures decided to take a
crescent shaped, somewhat out of the way route

through mostly uninhabited areas and attack Jerusalem from the southeast. This would greatly surprise the defenders since they would be looking for any attack to come from the Mediterranean.

They surfaced in the Med and noted the full moon was obscured by clouds. It was a dark night, luck was with them. They wouldn't be so easy to detect. Since this would be the third attack, they knew this time the humans would probably be ready in advance to broadcast their attack live on their TV networks. This was part of their plan; they wanted them to witness what they were going to do. The twin terrors wanted all of them to get a good look at this and finally understand how useless it was trying to stop them.

As a result they decided they would time their approach and use the darkness to mask their movement to the city. Then with the sunrise and in full view of the humans they would carry out their attack. They relished the idea that all the humans would see this event even if they weren't physically there. Of course a lot of this depended on if the humans were smart enough to figure out Alpha's taunting words in New York City. Well it makes no difference, the dye is cast now. If they don't broadcast this one there's always the next.

They moved quickly but quietly, giving as wide a berth as possible to any towns they encountered. Most of the working people in the small towns were blissfully asleep as they quietly passed. Whenever a large town or city, with all their annoying lights, crossed their path they made an extra wide swing around it. All of their detours slowed their progress. They were still 15 miles from the ancient city when the approaching sun began to remove the mask of darkness. They were not concerned however with the sunrise. At least they had avoided the irritating blasts and noise from the human's weapons for most of their journey.

As they passed a small town an early rising citizen was out stretching his legs on his early morning walk. He was startled to see the incredible sight of the two large beasts briskly walking by off in the distance. He reached for his cell phone but to his chagrin he didn't have it on him. He had absentmindedly left it at home. He turned and ran, then after tiring walked quickly back to his house to alert someone to his terrifying discovery. Twenty minutes later he was on the phone breathlessly telling what he saw to the local police.

After initial skepticism one of the policemen began to try to take a report from the confused and emotional voice on the other end of the line. Another officer went outside and drove to the outskirts in an attempt to get a clear view. He didn't see anything except a little dust. The creatures had cleared the area by the time he had arrived and there was nothing to see. Despite repeated questioning the caller insisted there were two animals walking together not one. This was in direct contradiction to what they were told was the threat by the government. They were told it was a single animal, not two. The two policemen thought about trashing the report, but because of the heightened level of alert in the country they decided to pass it on to higher channels. In spite of their reservations they decided to send the report as it was and let others make what they will of it.

In the headquarters for the defense of Jerusalem the curious report was received and analyzed. When it was noted there were supposedly two creatures instead of one and the sighting was from the southeast, the eyewitness account was dismissed along with the other false alarms. They were receiving them just about every ten minutes or so. No alerts were given or was the security level raised. It was considered just another false alarm.

Twenty five minutes later an army recon unit spotted the two huge beasts walking rapidly toward Jerusalem. They immediately got on their radios and sent out the alarm. In their excitement and surprise to see such a sight however, their radio discipline was poor. It took them several minutes to properly report the location, direction of travel, speed and a description of the two adversaries.

The alert was sent out to all military units and to the entire world. The creature was in Israel and almost upon the city of Jerusalem. Also in one of the most shocking and unanticipated developments possible, there were now two of them to deal with not just one. All over a stunned world military and civilian communications channels sprung to life. This was a story with worldwide interest and all the nations on the globe had a stake in it. In every country news bulletins were flashed on all media announcing the shocking events in the Middle East. All over the world people searched TV channels, their computers, cell phones and tablets looking for any coverage of the monumental happenings.

In the office of Prime Minister Ben-Gurion he was both relieved and apprehensive. He was relieved that his instincts were right and all the waiting was now over. But he also was apprehensive and a little fearful about the outcome that awaited his country and the world this day. All of their preparation and planning may prove naught and this whole affair may prove a complete catastrophe. Well, it's all in God's hands now, he thought.

In the Atlanta headquarters of SNN Robert Dayton's phone was ringing. A quick glance at the caller ID told him it was SNN's owner and CEO, William Fentress. He rolled his eyes to the ceiling. What does he want? I don't have time for this now, I'm too busy.

"Hello this is Robert Dayton speaking."

He spoke to the CEO as if he didn't know it was him on the line.

"Robert, who do we have to cover this story in Jerusalem?"

In typical Fentress fashion he went straight to the point skipping the pleasantries and not even giving his name.

"Oh, Mister Fentress," Dayton acted surprised. "How are you doing today? Luckily for us we have a reporter on location in Jerusalem, Miss Elisha Washington."

"Elisha Washington, who's that?"

"You remember her sir, she's the one who first reported on this thing a while back in Ashanti."

"Oh, yeah I remember her now, but what's she doing there? I saw the list you made and I didn't see her name on it or anyone assigned to Jerusalem as a matter of fact."

"Well sir that's true on the original report I sent you but I added her and the city to a revised and updated report. I sent it to you several weeks later. Did you get the latest list, Mr. Fentress?"

"Who knows, I get so many reports I can't keep track of them all. Whose bright idea was it to put her there anyway? Can she handle this? I don't have to tell you how big this story is to our network."

"Actually I picked her for this assignment myself and I'm confident she will do an outstanding job for the network."

"Well she better, it looks like we don't have any other horse we can run today. When are we going live? All I see now is filler and old footage."

"Any minute now, I'm sorry sir but I have to go now. As you can imagine it's pretty hectic around here right now."

"Ok Robert let me know if then is anything I can do to help. Goodbye."

"Goodbye, Mr. Fentress."

As Dayton hung up he was a little confused. Was that it? The irritating and obnoxious control freak that was William Fentress let him go that easily? Not only that, he genuinely sounded like he wanted to be helpful at the end of their conversation. Maybe the world is in worse shape than he realized. It really must be coming to an end when Fentress starts sounding considerate to his subordinates.

The beehive of activity had slowly come to a halt in front of the Wailing Wall area. Everything and everyone was in their assigned place. It was unnaturally quiet now, no sounds were heard except for a priest loudly praying and pacing back and forth on the wall. The scene was in sharp contrast to the earlier shouting and frantic movement.

The preparations for defense were all prepared on the logical assumption that the attack would come from the most direct route from the sea, which would be west of the city. For this reason most of the defenses were positioned in that direction to repel such an attack. After all it was just an animal and all its previous appearances came directly from the sea. Now having to quickly modify their plans at the last minute, the commanders of the Jerusalem defense had to scramble to redeploy their units. They had to face a southern threat now and the reality of two creatures instead of one. Most of their artillery units were positioned in the wrong direction and out of range rendering them useless. The Air Force had no such limitations and sprang into action. Waves of F-35's launched from their bases and headed for the last known position of the creature. Their orders were to attack whenever there was an opportunity as long as the target wasn't in a densely populated area.

While there were local networks in the country broadcasting live, SNN was the only worldwide network at the site. They had accomplished a tremendous coup with their gamble and was the only network broadcasting the story to the world live. Their risky strategy had paid off and with their basic monopoly on this story the whole world was tuned to their channel. Back at the Wailing Wall location of SNN's coverage the network was returning to the live broadcast of Miss Washington after a series of long commercial breaks.

"This is Elisa Washington reporting for SNN live at the Wailing Wall. Everything seems calm for now. You would hardly belief a huge drama is about to take place here. This city has seen its share of war and destruction but nothing like this has ever taken place here. The Israelis are convinced this location is the target of the two creatures and have arranged their defensive strategy based on that assumption. We are going to broadcast from here as long as possible but if it becomes too dangerous we are going to have to move to another location. If I can get the camera to pan around the area I would like to show you what is happening here."

Her cameraman slowly panned his camera around the sight stopping whenever Leesh was keying on a specific point in the background.

"If you notice there are what look like large

caliber machine guns mounted on and at different points of the wall. They also are mounted at different points around the courtyard and on the top of nearby buildings. They also have them mounted on the old city walls. A lot of them mounted on the west city wall are aimed in the wrong direction however and are now being moved in a frantic effort to face south. We can't see what's happening at the southern city wall, but curiously for some reason most of the guns we see in all the areas seem to be unmanned for now. They look to be prepared and ready to fire but no troops are manning them right now. You may notice the large tent is still there. Earlier we showed you the wheeled vehicles rushing out of the huge tent and roaring out of the city to head south. They each had an automatic weapon, presumably the same type that will be used in this area attached to them. Evidently they are going to confront the creatures in some sort of moving battle in the more open area to the south. Most experts we have talked to see no chance at all guns will have any effect on the animals and feel the Israelis are foolishly wasting their time and effort on these tactics. That at least explains some of what was under the tent. But the tent is still standing for some reason. There may be something else under there that they haven't revealed yet."

The roar of jets came from the sky as formations of aircraft passed overhead. The camera panned skyward.

"As you can see viewers, waves of what appear to be F-35's are flying past the city and are headed south, apparently to attack the creatures."

As the attack jets roared past the city and headed for the target the pilots were confident they were going to hit their target. They were well trained and experienced in the art of war through numerous wars and conflicts. They were not so sure however they were going to destroy their enemy. They had seen the video of the monstrous terror absorb hit after hit of high explosives and not even flinch. They were determined to do their best but they feared for the fate that awaited their country. Now there on the horizon the two beasts could be seen. The strike commander radioed in his position and gave the order to attack.

Back at the city and at Leesh's position a distant thumping could be heard like the sound of thunder a long way off. First one then another, with increasing tempo the deep sounding roar increased. But it wasn't thunder this day but the sound of bombs and rockets exploding in the distance. And another thing was noticeable; the sounds were slowly getting louder and closer.

CHAPTER 27

The F-35 pilots had done their part. Out of ordinance and with the creatures approaching more populated areas they turned for home. Their weapons had no effect on the targets. They just kept on walking through all of the attacks with an almost distain for their antagonists, the jets.

Now it will be up to the Army, there is nothing else the Air Force can do, thought the strike commander.

The SNN crew had sent the only other camera and cameraman they had to a point over the horizon to try to get footage of the titanic events. The creatures were now close enough to their vantage point that they were able to get grainy but viewable images of the two animals approaching in the distance. Eerily all over the world viewers which were now glued to their screens saw two monsters, seemingly walking unopposed toward a major city. Their only opposition seemed to be an occasional few puffs of smoke from a few artillery pieces whose rounds had found the range. Most of the artillery was unable to reposition in time to try to halt the creatures advance.

As a result of the instance urging of SNN headquarters Leesh and her crew pulled back to a safer distance from the presumed target, the Wailing

Wall. But who knows if they're going to stop there, she thought. The first one said he was going to remove a burdensome stone. He could be talking about the whole city and there could be no safe place anywhere.

For the first time today Leesh began to feel fear and the thought that she could die today covering this story. But then she remembered Pastor Warren's words to her. She was supposed to be here. Surely God didn't put me here to die; I'm here to report and bear witness to these events. No matter what happens I'm going to do exactly that.

Back on the field of battle, which was anywhere the creatures stepped foot now, the twin terrors were making their way closer and closer to the city. To them the human flying machines had finished their attack and had left in defeat. Nothing the attackers had could get past their all powerful force fields. Now that the humans had used their best weapons to no affect it should be a cakewalk now to destroy their objective.

As they traveled in a large open area the creatures were both startled and slightly amused to see small four wheeled vehicles racing toward them leaving streams of dust in their wake. They each had what looked like machine guns mounted on them. Have the humans lost their minds? Do they think their pea shooters can do any harm to us?

The creatures figured such a pathetic attempt is not even worth the time it would take to fight it. They reasoned there's no need to waste energy using their shields. Their armored scales will have no trouble stopping bullets. Unless the humans got too close with their vehicles they were simply going to ignore them.

As soon as they were in range the mobile units

opened fire. They poured round after round into the two animals. They turned, wheeled and circled the two huge beasts scoring hit after hit. The two animals were being raked from head to tail but nothing seemed to happen. They simply walked on as if they were out for a stroll. To the Israelis surprise they didn't even try to fight back but seemed to greet their efforts with contempt.

They were approaching houses now and the mobile units decided to press their attack more aggressively. In lei of any response they came in closer and closer with their circling and darting attacks, firing continuously.

Every now and then a crew would press his attack too closely and one of the animals reached out and crushed the vehicle or smacked it completely off the ground launching it into the air. The resulting effect was the death of the three person crew which greatly pleased the creatures. The crews reported the animals seemed to have a happy expression on their faces when they did this almost as if they enjoyed destroying the vehicles. But of course this had to be wrong reasoned the people who hear the reports. No animal enjoys killing, they had to be making the normal human mistake of assigning human traits to animals.

As the creatures entered a housing area the mobile units backed off and waited for them to clear the houses. The soldiers didn't want to risk the lives of the people in the houses. They waited for them to clear the housing area before resuming their attack. While they were waiting they tested, serviced and rearmed their weapons. They also took time to assess their situation. They started out as a force of twelve but were down to eight because of damage to their vehicles in the wild driving campaign and attacks by the monsters. Their weapons were working well and they still had plenty of the special rounds. Unfortunately despite repeated hits they saw no evidence they were causing any damage to the targets. They were determined to continue their attacks however, for as long as possible.

As the two animals cleared the houses the vehicles shadowed them until they were a reasonable distance from the housing area. With that accomplished, they accelerated rapidly and resumed their twisting and turning attacks. They continued to rake the two animals with continuous fire but as before the animals continued to mostly ignore them. The seemly one sided battle was now reaching the valley of Hinnom. Many people refer to this as the valley of Gehenna or Hell. In biblical times it was a sight where Jerusalem's garbage was disposed of in ever burning fires.

The creatures paused before stepping down the rocky ground into the valley of Hell. They could see the domes of the mosques near the Wall and the whole city in front of them. They were close now and nothing could stop them. They walked gingerly on the rocky ground and down into the valley. They were met by a fierce barrage of automatic weapons fire from the mobile units which had managed to get in front of them. The vehicles had taken an easier route into the valley and maneuvered to a point ahead of the creatures.

With the old city walls behind them the units changed their strategy. The enemy was almost upon the city so the hit and run strategy was over, now it was time for desperation. The units needed to get the maximum amount of firepower on the two targets. They formed up line abreast and slowly retreated toward the city. Staying out of easy grasp of the animals they engulfed them with constant fire. Every gun was firing and every gun was hitting the targets, but the creatures continued to walk toward them with no concern for what they considered their puny efforts.

Back at the city Leesh continued her reporting. The remote cameraman, while keeping a somewhat safe distance from the action, was able to broadcast most of the action as the fighting left the housing area.

"Viewers as you have seen this is about to become one of the most tragic days in history or at least in this century. The military has shared with us that all of the ammunition being fired today by the army are special rounds developed especially for use on the creatures. The details of the ammunition have not been disclosed to us but they seemed to have developed them in secret unbeknown to the rest of the world. Questions on how they did this and what makes them think they would have any success were not answered. That explains why there are so many machine guns here. They are set up around the Wall and in front of the southern old city wall."

Leesh pushed her earpiece further into her ear to hear an off camera remark from one of her colleagues.

"I am told now they are not machine guns but automatic cannons. I must say no matter what they are they don't seem to be working. The creatures are not being deterred by them and are steadily advancing on the city. It seems like they're heading for the area of the old city wall that has the Dung Gate. That would be the most direct route to the Wailing Wall and may confirm the Israelis belief that is where they are headed. There is no way they could fit through that gate but I doubt that any wall or gate will stop them. They have shown they will simply smash through it."

Through her earpiece she was told it was time for another commercial break. How ridiculous, with the faith of mankind on the line the network is still worried about making money. Or as Mr. Fentress would say, reporting the news is nice, but the advertisers pay the bills.

"We'll be back in a few minutes with exclusive live coverage of these tragic events. This is Elisha Washington reporting from Jerusalem."

The creatures were however unconcerned with commercials or station breaks or anything else the humans hold dear. They were now becoming annoyed with the constant stream of fire directed at them from the mobile units. The city walls were in sight now and in a little while they would repay these particular humans with the destruction of what they considered priceless and irreplaceable. They would destroy their precious Wailing Wall and then before they left they would take out the mosques and anything else on the Temple Mount sight. They only wished the second Temple was still there, they would have loved to smash that and hear the whining of these humans. Oh well they thought, but you can't have everything.

CHAPTER 28

From her vantage point near the Wall Leesh saw soldiers running over to the huge tent. Something was beginning to happen and they were still in the commercial break. With grim satisfaction she pulled the plug on the commercial using the prearranged code for breaking news. When this was used anything that was on the air was killed and a live broadcast was always immediately returned to the air.

"Something is about to happen with the huge tent in the courtyard. It looks like soldiers are about to take the tent down."

The young reported began a running description of what was happening in the courtyard. Suddenly at a prearranged signal, men all around the tent removed the poles and ropes holding the tent. In an obviously rehearsed and choreographed move they lifted and collapsed the tent in such a way that the contents in the tent were not touched. A loud gasp went out from all the people in the area at the sight that they witnessed. There in the courtyard were standing four dozen or so troops at rigid attention. But they were not dressed like any troops anyone had ever seen, at least not in centuries. Speaking over the noise of the constant gunfire from the battle which was getting louder as it moved closer, Leesh continued her narration.

"This is truly amazing. I hope you people all around the world are getting a good view of this scene. These soldiers standing at attention in the courtyard are exquisitely dressed in what I would describe as battle outfits that would have been worn over two thousand years ago. They are standing there wearing metal helmets and holding metal shields. The sun is reflecting off the polished surfaces giving a brilliant and spectacular effect to the whole scene. They are also each wearing a sword hanging from their waist and some of them have spears. Curiously the soldiers with the spears also have what look like machine guns slung on their shoulders."

"All of this looks magnificent but how any of this will help the current situation is a mystery. Now as you see they are breaking ranks and groups are running to man the guns mounted all around the area. A dozen of them with the spears have formed two rows and are kneeling down in the courtyard. This has all the markings of what looks like a last stand to protect the Wall. This is unbelievable, these men are surely facing suicide but they seem calm and relaxed about the whole thing. I hope they have orders to evacuate the area before the creatures reach here but somehow I don't think that is their plan."

As the two terrors neared the southern old city wall they came in range of the guns in front of and on the wall. The mobile units were between them and the guns at the wall. The vehicles separated into two groups and quickly took positions on both sides of the animals. The guns at the wall opened up a furious barrage and the vehicles opened up from both sides. The creatures were now caught in a crossfire and were being hit from three directions. But they continued on with no concern other than annoyance with all the fireworks.

A spotter on the roof of a nearby tall building was closely studying the two animals when he thought he noticed something odd about the one called Omega. He adjusted his scope for maximum magnification and zeroed in on the suspicious area. He was correct, there was something running down the side of the creature and he could swear it almost looked like blood. He blinked, rubbed, cleared his eyes and took a second look. It was blood; the one on the left was bleeding and had to be wounded. He quickly reported this development to HQ with his helmet mounted radio.

The creatures continued on completely unaware anything was happening. They had an approximation of an animal body but the machine that created them didn't give them nerves that could feel pain. It considered that unimportant so nerves were left out. As a result if they were ever hurt they would not feel anything. A roar went out from the troops as word was sent to them that one of the creatures was wounded. The mobile units nearest to Omega became more embolden at the news and pressed their attacks closer. As a result one of them exploded in a huge fireball after being crushed in a sudden lunge by Omega. Undaunted they continued to press their furious and desperate attacks. They felt a bloodlust now and sensed they were on the verge of a kill.

"I don't know what all the cheering and shouting is about, but it seems something has happened," said Leesh.

"Wait a minute; I'm getting something from our control booth. This is unbelievable; the army is reporting one of the creatures is wounded and bleeding. From our vantage point and as you can see on camera we can't confirm that. In fact we don't see them acting any differently. They're still coming but the mobile units on the left seem to have moved in much closer on the left creature. The creature on the left must be the one they think is wounded. It appears they are making a concentrated effort to bring that one down."

As the defenders continued to pour out fire Omega suddenly stumbled and fell on one knee. Alpha continued on for a few paces then turned to look back in shock and confusion to see what was wrong. He rushed over to his companion and to his great surprise he saw blood streaming out the side of Omega. This is impossible. This can't be happening. Nothing can hurt us.

"One of the creatures is down," shouted Leesh into her microphone.

Quickly composing herself she lowered the tone of her voice and continued her narration.

"The wounded animal seems to be seriously wounded and is down on one knee. Somehow the Israelis have found a way to hurt them or at least one of them."

Alpha quickly activated his force field around his body and Omega did the same. Now his companion had dropped down to all fours and was breathing heavily. He was in serious distress now and his eyes were half closed. Omega couldn't maintain his weak force field and it faltered.

Damn these devious humans, thought Alpha. Is there no end to their scheming? Somehow they figured out a way to get past our scales. I underestimated them once again; I'll never fight them again without my shield at full power.

Abruptly the wounded beast rolled over on its side in his final ballet of death. Alpha let out a loud

258

roar of outrage and frustration. He made a quick dash to the nearest vehicles quickly smashing one and tossing the other high into the air. The men in the vehicles were thrown out in midair and the angry beast ran over to the bodies and quickly ate them. Two of the men thrown out were still alive and died screaming as they were taken up into the horrible jaws. He turned to get more vehicles but the rest quickly moved out of range. They were faster than him on land and he couldn't seem to catch them.

Suddenly there was a large glow surrounding the dying Omega. He was energy turned to matter but he was rapidly losing the ability to control that energy. He was now in the process of turning from matter back to pure energy. The glow increased until it was almost as bright as the noon day sun. Everyone, including Alpha stopped what they were doing and stared at the unfolding scene. Suddenly there was a huge bolt of energy like a lightning bolt shooting up into the sky. Omega's energy was set free and it was sent to the heavens. Nothing was left but a large burned out scorch on the ground.

There was not a sound on the battlefield, and everyone was still staring at the spot where Omega once laid. The defenders quickly broke the calm and once again opened up with a barrage of gunfire. Alpha, now outraged at the demise of his cohort, made up his mind that the humans would pay dearly for this affront. He was going to only destroy the Wall and the Temple Mount area at first, but now he is going to destroy the whole city in reprisal. With a new sense of purpose he resumed his trek toward the Dung Gate absorbing tremendously increased gunfire. With only one beast to target now the defenders didn't have to divide their fire. All of their gunfire was aimed at Alpha, so now in effect the volume reaching him doubled.

Undaunted, the lone beast made short work of the distance to the city wall, treating the human's gunfire with all the respect he had for it - - none. He swiftly silenced the gunfire from the southern wall, raking the irritating guns in front of him with his large clawed paws. The humans, who manned their posts and kept firing until the end, were smashed along with their guns. His rake of the wall left a satisfying red smear along the surface from the blood of the defenders. He enjoyed the look of his handiwork, but his payback was only just beginning.

He began his destruction of the Dung Gate by ripping and tearing apart the stones. In less than a minute, he had almost enough room to squeeze through with his body. Without waiting to finish he simply squeezed through the opening he made knocking down the wall sections on either side of him. As he entered the old city he was greeted by more gunfire from positions in nearby buildings. With his all powerful force field in place he was not concerned with their feeble defenses. Now it was time to exact his vengeance. He stopped to get his bearings ignoring the loud pointblank fire from nearby buildings around him. He could see the large shining dome in front of him and he knew he was near his first objective.

Leesh and her cameraman, who were still broadcasting, had a perfect view of the action from a nearby building. In a somewhat lowered voice, almost as if she feared the creature would hear and attack her vantage point, she described the scene.

"As you can see and hear, the loud bark of gunfire is almost constant as the animal is being hit from all directions. He is standing very close to our location and just seems to be looking around, as if he

is planning his next move. There seems to be a slight
- - very slight glow around him. One of our military
advisors says it's his understanding the creature has
the ability to put some kind of force field around him
for protection and that is what we may be seeing.
They say this wasn't observed previous to the first
one being killed, so I would say the chances of killing
this one with their special weapons would appear
slim. There … he's starting to move again and is
heading down a street leading to the Wailing Wall.
The creature is headed down a main street that is
much wider than most of the others in this area. It
looks like the final pages of this tragic day are about
to be written, and it doesn't look good for the city of
Jerusalem. This could very well be the final chapter
in the long history of this city."

He took the most direct route he could to the
Wall, as he smashed any structures in his way. He
seemed to be greeted by gunfire at almost every turn.
And now the worrisome mobile vehicles were back.
Taking a different route into the city, they had once
again gotten in front of him and were adding their fire
to the fray. The city defenders seemed determined to
fight to the end. Well so am I and I spit on their
efforts.

Now, with only two city blocks to go, he was
almost upon his target in spite of all the gunfire. His
primary goal and victory over the humans was in
sight. But as he stepped on a large truck in his way
he almost lost his balance. His almost fall was broken
by him slamming into a nearby building crumbling it in
the process. Odd, he thought.

As he continued on, he seemed to have more
and more trouble keeping his balance. What in the
world is going on?

He looked down at himself and was

dumbfounded at what he saw, he was bleeding.

This is impossible, thought the towering menace. I have my force field out and nothing has the power to get through my force field.

Down at the Wall, the specially equipped troops moved from the area directly in front of the wall and formed a blocking formation directly in the path of the creature. They armed and readied their weapons. This was it; now was the time to either win or die. There was no other option available to them.

Another huge cheer went out from the soldiers and the foolhardy civilians who had snuck through roadblocks and barriers to get a look at history. Word had come that this last one was now bleeding and wounded.

The defiant animal was still determined to destroy his primary objective, the Wall, however. He announced to the world he was going to do it, and he was still going to do it. Maybe then he could retreat to the desert and renew himself in the blazing sun and heat. He continued on using the sheer force of his will. Only one city block to go now and then it will be done.

Seeing that he was close enough, the special troops took aim and opened fire, adding their firepower to the barrage. The creature stopped momentarily at the sudden new blast and for a second, almost looked like he was starting to sway backward. But, he began to move forward again although much slower. Every step now seemed laborious; and he seemed to be slowing more with each step. Fire continued to pour in, and then dramatically he stopped. His eyes seemed to roll back in his head and he fell to the pavement only 300 feet from the Wall. A cheer went up from the crowd but he was not dead. He was however, breathing heavily and laboriously in the street with no other visible signs of movement. All of the gunfire suddenly stopped as everyone stared at the sight.

Then spontaneously and without direction, one of special troops threw down his automatic weapon and his spear. With a loud yell, he drew his sword and raised it holding it to the sky. He then broke ranks and ran toward the creature lying on the ground with sword in hand. First, one then another of the soldiers did the same thing, and in quick order the entire unit was racing down the street to the animal, screaming with swords raised. When they reached the creature, there was a frenzied flurry of cutting, hacking, and stabbing. Apparently, he had lost the ability to hold his force field, and the integrity of his scales had been compromised.

The swords, which everyone assumed to only be ceremonial, turned out to be razor sharp and the troops found no problem getting between the scales with them. As they hit them they began to fall off, exposing more of the underlying surface to attack. The creature had no ability left in him to focus or even fight back and absorbed blow after blow. After several minutes of this butchery and bloodbath, several of the soldiers brought an end to this by decapitating the animal's head from his body.

Suddenly a bright glow started to form around him, just as it did before with Omega and the attackers ran from the beast, leaving him to his fate. Once again, everyone shielded their eyes as the glow brightened to rival that of the sun. Lightning rose from the ground, heading skyward once again and there was nothing left of the creature except a huge dark spot on the pavement. The city, the country, and mankind were saved by the most unlikely series of events anyone could imagine.

EPILOGUE

Several weeks after the climactic battle in Jerusalem, the Prime Minister of Israel was enjoying lunch with his old friend, Rabbi Isaac Peled. The world had seemingly returned to normal, or, at the least, back to standard day-to-day activity. The series of events that led up to the battle, however, had changed the world forever.

"Well Daniel, things worked out well. Your special weapon turned out to actually work against the beast, praise God."

"Did it? We did an in depth analysis of all the data and video that was recorded during the battle and I don't think we can take any credit for what happened."

"What do you mean?"

"Oh, there was a chance we may have gotten the first one. But, after looking at the video over and over, we couldn't find any evidence that the last animal was injured before he activated his force field. There was no blood or any evidence that he was injured until after he put up his energy field. My experts tell me there is no way our rounds could have gotten through his force field. That, they weren't designed to do. So, none of our shots could have caused the injuries that disabled the last one."

"Amazing, well then that means…"

"Yes, that means God answered our prayers, and He delivered us. This is what many people are already saying. They didn't wait for a scientific analysis to tell them. They just believed that God would deliver them . . . and He did."

"I must say, Daniel, the mood of the country has really changed. More and more people are returning to prayer and faith as a result of this. I've never seen anything like this in my lifetime. People are reading the scriptures and questioning everything, even our old assumptions."

"Yes I understand there has been a move back to faith."

"Oh, it's gone way past that now. More people are now even questioning our long held belief that the Messiah hasn't come yet."

"What do you mean?"

"An offshoot of this new faith movement is a lot of people are saying we were wrong about a lot of things, like thinking we could save ourselves; so, maybe we have been wrong about everything. They are saying, 'after all, most of the world seems to believe the Messiah was Jesus, and he has already been here.' Many are saying, 'maybe they are right and we should at least consider the possibility'."

"Oh my God, what have I started?" asked the Prime Minister smiling and in slightly mock fashion. Then he turned serious once again. "I do think the end of this story hasn't been written yet. And who can say but God how this whole thing is going to turn out."

All over the world more people were coming to that same conclusion. Something enormous had happened. Mankind had been humbled and sent to the brink in a way it had never before experienced. As a result the world would never be the same again.